WHAT HAUNTS US

A Colin Vale Novella

C. Perez

Trigger Warning: This story includes dialouge and situations that contain bigotry, homophobia, slut-shaming, racist language, and child endangerment. Sorry friends, our villian is a real piece of work.

For all my seasonal depression baddies: may these pages haunt you kindly and make the dark nights a little softer.

CONTENTS

CHAPTER 1

WILL

The scream sliced through Will like a hot knife.

"Colin?!" His voice cracked, desperate at his little brother's shriek.

The sound had been shrill and filled with a terror that made Will abandon all caution. He bolted across the open space, lungs burning, cobwebs tearing against his jacket, the beam from his flashlight swinging wildly. The air was stale and thick with mildew and something animal. Beneath his boots, the warped floorboards groaned, one sagging ominously and pitching him into the shadows.

At the far end of the attic, Colin stood rigid as a statue, one of his hands clamped over his opposite forearm so tightly that his knuckles were bone-white. His cheeks flushed, fever-bright, and his grey-blue eyes glared at where Julian was bent double.

Julian's long hair fell into his face as he gasped with raucous laughter. "Oh my God, Colin! That's a horror movie scream! I didn't know you had it in you!"

Colin's scowl was enough to melt steel. "It fucking scratched me, you dick."

Will screeched to a halt, his heart still pounding. "Scratched? What?" He closed the distance between them and tugged at Colin's iron grip until the other man's arm came free. Four livid lines slashed down the pale skin of his inner forearm, raised and angry, but shallow. "What the hell?"

Colin's gaze darted to where Lance and Grace were crouching over an open steamer trunk. From inside came the frantic scuffle and high-pitched chitter of small creatures.

"Raccoons," Colin said, grimacing.

"Mama raccoon was not happy to see Colin," Julian said, wheezing with mirth. He wiped his dark eyes dramatically. "I nearly pissed myself! Christ, Col!"

Colin flipped him off without hesitation. Will ignored them both and dug a handkerchief from his back pocket to dab at the scratches, jaw tight.

Grace was already on her phone, her voice calm as she relayed directions to a wildlife rescue. Dust clung to her curls like powdered sugar, streaking the messy twist of hair at the nape of her neck. She caught Will's eye and gave him a brief nod to say, 'It's handled,' and returned to her work. Will's shoulders eased a fraction.

"I'll go downstairs and assure the family there's no ghost, just raccoons," Lance said. His brown eyes shone with mirth, bu he had the good grace to keep his amusement to himself. "Rescue should be able to move the critters safely."

Colin took over tending his own arm, sheepish now that the adrenaline had passed. Will exhaled hard, raking a hand through his hair. "Raccoons," he said, pinching the bridge of his nose.

"Jesus Christ. I thought something had attacked you."

"Something *did* attack me," Colin retorted, bristling. His shoulders drooped and his eyes were rimmed with dark circles, a clear sign he hadn't been sleeping well. When he was younger, he'd come to Will with his concerns, his nightmares, but lately he'd been clammed up and unwilling to discuss whatever was wrong.

Will hated it. All of it. Colin's mysterious gifts and the impassable wall that it created between them. He couldn't see, couldn't share the burden. He could only stand there, fists clenched, patching his brother up when the world clawed at him.

"Well, I feel accomplished," Julian quipped, gesturing broadly at the box where the raccoon kits huddled like guilty culprits. "Mystery solved! Go Team Haunt Hunters!"

Will's patience frayed. "We're not using that name, you—" He stopped, eyes on Colin, who had suddenly slumped against his side. His gaze lingered upward, scanning the rafters where the shadows pooled thickest. For a long moment, he was elsewhere, listening to something Will couldn't hear.

"Col? You with me?"

There was no response, just that terrible awareness etched into every line of his face. The raccoons scrabbled and squeaked, oblivious to the chaos they'd caused.

By the time the group had made it downstairs to join Lance and the "haunted family" who'd hired them, the wildlife truck was pulling into the drive. Headlights sliced across slats of the house, making the two story farmhouse look ominous and looming. Metal cages clanked in the back of the rescue van, and the bark of a dog carried from somewhere down the street. The family lingered nervously on the veranda, half-relieved, half-embarrassed.

Julian was still riding high, arms crossed, and a grin plastered across his face. He rocked on his heels in the glow of the porch lamp as they began loading the van and packing up their equipment. "Right," he declared, tone dripping with mischief, "so if we split this fairly, I get thirty percent, Colin gets a sympathetic scratch allowance, and the rest of you can divvy up the other fifty."

Colin pinned him with a look acidic enough to strip paint. Exhaustion still lined his face, but a familiar spark of stubbornness flared in his eyes. Will smiled. It was the same spark that had carried them through schoolyard bullies and sleepless nights chasing shadows throughout their childhood.

"I think we should donate the rest for conservation," Grace interrupted without looking up, her thumbs flying across her phone. Several curls had slipped free of her twist now, clinging to the ebony skin of her neck and forehead in soft, dust-streaked ringlets. The blue glow of her screen reflected off her glasses like beacons. "Local sanctuaries always need funds. We could sponsor a small enclosure for raccoon kits."

Will shook his head, ignoring the argument that was sure to follow such a suggestion and instead tugged Colin forward to inspect his arm in better lighting. The skin was angry and red, but the scratches didn't look deep. Still, his pulse hadn't slowed since the scream. "I swear, Colin, you get injured no matter where we go. You're lucky those claws didn't pierce deeper. Thank God you've had your shots." He retrieved the first-aid kit and began tying a clean wrap around his brother's arm with quick, practiced motions, tucking the end under with a huff.

Colin made a face. "You're such a mother hen."

"Well, somebody has to look out for you, you idiot, so I'll take that as a compliment." Will shot back, relief softening his tone.

Lance drifted into their orbit then, shifting from foot to foot with his hands shoved deep in his jacket pockets. Their little ghost-hunting team was a hobbyist group at best, formed organically through Colin's strange and often terrifying abilities. They lacked consistent work, but sometimes the world called out to Colin, and he always answered.

When Lance started dating Grace, he'd jumped at the opportunity to be involved and helpful, taking over their social media and website and helping them to book more consistent jobs that offered actual payment. Lance had only done three investigations with them so far, but he was a blissfully grounding presence, a nice counterpoint to Julian's boisterousness and Colin's intensity.

He cleared his throat. "I think I have our next case." The words froze the group mid-motion. Even Julian, who was still arguing about the profit split, mostly to wind Grace up into a tangent.

"Go on," Will said, dusting off his sleeve while keeping Colin in his periphery. The younger man was leaning against the side of their van now, obvious fatigue pulling him sideways.

"It's a friend of mine, actually. Arthur Ashford. He's a coworker. His sister inherited their family home and moved in with her son. They've had... strange things. Arthur doesn't believe in the supernatural, but his sister's convinced."

Will's brow pinched. "What kind of strange?"

"Objects moving. Flickering lights. Noises. And the boy..." Lance hesitated, searching for words. "The boy's been off. Arthur says it's stress. But he was unsettled enough to ask me to come by so—"

"Wait! Ashford?" Julian lit up like a slot machine. "As in Land-Tycoon August Ashford? Oh, mate. We could charge double!" His grin gleamed, shameless.

Will groaned, arms crossing. "I'd rather not get involved in a family dispute. If she wants us, why is the brother the one calling it in?"

Lance shrugged. "I think they're just desperate. And scared."

Will's gaze cut instinctively to Colin, who had gone utterly still, like a prey animal trying to go unnoticed. He locked his jaw and his body tightened like wire. Will's stomach turned. He'd seen that look before, too many times. He knew something was up, but Colin stubbornly refused to meet his eyes and divulge his thoughts.

Julian, oblivious or willfully ignorant, clapped his hands together. "Scared and rich is my favorite combination. Rich people love throwing money at their problems. Come on, this is the best opportunity we could ask for. Think of the payday!"

Colin's fingers tapped against the bandage on his arm, his entire frame vibrating with unease and indecision.

"Colin," Grace pressed, voice velvet but with steel underneath, "if there's a child involved…"

"Fuck." Colin groaned, dragging both hands down his face. In that moment, he looked ten years older, worn down by too many long, sleepless nights. "You're right," he sighed. "If there's a kid, we can't ignore it."

Julian whooped, throwing a fist in the air. "That's the spirit! Just think of the payday!"

Will let out a slow breath, his jaw tightening. "Colin's already agreed, Jules, you can stop now."

Julian grinned wolfishly and gave a mock salute as he turned to jog around the front of the van and get it started. Grace tucked her phone away, turning that soft smile toward Colin. "We'll be careful," she promised, her tone the kind that always made Will unclench, if only a fraction.

Lance shifted closer. "I can handle security," he said, voice soft as he took in Will's obviously disappointed expression. "If you really don't want to go, I mean. I can handle it. I already know Arthur and—"

"Colin's not stepping foot in that house without me."

The words dropped between them like an oath. Colin's gaze found his then, blue eyes weary but touched, the corner of his mouth twitching with appreciation.

Will's chest tightened, dread choking him, but if Colin was going, he was. There was no question. He'd follow him anywhere, even into Hell.

CHAPTER 2

GRACE

The apartment was small, and with all of them crammed inside, it was bursting at the seams. Gear leaned across various furniture in lopsided stacks, threatening to topple. The thrift-store couch they'd carried up to the third floor together years ago sagged under her and Lance's combined weight, and the fridge hummed in the background like it was generating electricity for the block and not sub-standard food preservation.

Grace shifted against Lance's shoulder and let his warmth relax the tension in her spine. She was cross-eyed from trying to verify land documents in the new Ashford case.

Colin, with his long limbs and slender build, perched on the other seat of the couch. He easily squeezed into the too-small space and folded his legs and arms against himself like a baby giraffe.

In the kitchen, Will was humming loudly and off-key, pots and pans banging a staccato. He always cooked like someone feeding an army, though there were only five of them, and Grace wondered if he knew how to make less than a mountain of food.

Julian had taken over his usual spot in the old armchair, sprawling with deliberate drama, as if the battered upholstery were a throne. He was boasting loudly of his most recent conquest, a guy he'd met at the bar the night before.

Despite the apartment's clutter, chaos, and noise, Grace only ever felt comfort here. Years of shared history and a kind of scrappy affection had stitched them into a family.

She sometimes wondered how Will had managed to bring them all together. He'd only been seventeen years old when his parents died, and he found himself suddenly responsible for his traumatized twelve-year-old brother. He hadn't looked ready for it, not back then: too thin, too sharp around the edges, like he might splinter apart. But he hadn't. He'd stepped into the role without hesitation and with a stern word for anyone who had tried to talk him out of it.

She still remembered when the Vale brother's had first moved into the one-bedroom apartment in her building. Colin was quick to make friends, knocking on her door in search of a playmate his own age. He'd wasted little time before dragging her into his orbit and adventures. Her own parents had immediately started including both boys in their household's rhythms as if they had always been there. Will never said it out loud, but Grace knew he'd been lost that first year, and her family's kindness had given him something to hang onto.

Julian had come later, a spark thrown into their little trio. Will had dragged him in from the diner where they both worked, though nobody had expected him to stick the way he had.

The short-lived fling with Colin had been, in Will's words, "an unmitigated disaster," but Colin smiled more after it ended, not less. The romance had fizzled, but the friendship — loud, messy, and improbable — had settled in for good.

As Will came into the living room juggling bowls of boxed macaroni and passing them out, Grace took it all in and let herself breathe. This was the part that mattered; this was why they kept throwing themselves into dark basements and crumbling houses, why they risked sleepless nights and shadows that clung after the lights came back on. She could do something now, *help now*, to make some other family a little warmer and more stable.

She waited long enough for Will to settle cross-legged on the floor in front of Colin with his own heaping bowl of orange noodles before shattering the fragile peace that hung over the room. "Okay," she said, sitting up a little straighter. "The Ashford case."

Will groaned. Julian made a noise like a trumpet fanfare. Colin went white as printer paper.

Grace forged ahead anyway, pulling up the notes she'd been keeping on her computer, the cursor still blinking accusingly from where she'd been compiling details since her first call with Arthur Ashford. "Lance wasn't kidding when he said Arthur is a nonbeliever. He's convinced his sister and her son are unraveling. Trauma, hysteria, something a hospital should fix. He made it pretty clear that Alexandra was the one who had requested a paranormal team before they bailed out of the house altogether."

"It's a family estate, right?" Colin asked, raising his eyebrows but keeping his tone flat. "Why would it only start acting up now?"

Grace grimaced. "He didn't offer many details, but I got the impression that the Ashford children hadn't stepped foot in the place for years. They were apparently no-contact until lawyers called Alexandra to inform her of her father's death and her inheritance."

Will's frown deepened. "Sounds messy."

Grace pushed on, reading the words she'd typed but hearing Alexandra's voice instead: raw and desperate. "Arthur claims he hasn't seen much himself, but Alexandra's reported strange noises, cold spots. And her son, Theo—" her voice softened, unbidden "—Theo's been sickly. Withdrawn. He's ten. Arthur thinks it's the stress of moving, but…" She shook her head, throat tightening. "I'm worried about him."

Colin leaned forward, his long frame folding somehow impossibly more into itself. "A kid in a haunted house never ends well." His tone was too casual, but Grace saw the flicker in his eyes.

Lance crossed his arms, level-headed as always. "Let's not get ahead of ourselves. Old houses creak. Drafts make cold spots. Bad plumbing'll have a house moaning like a séance on its own."

"Could be mold," Will said pragmatically, spoon paused in mid-air. "Mold poisoning can make you lethargic and paranoid. Or the well. Contaminated water could explain why Theo's not himself."

Grace nodded along, but her stomach twisted hard against the simple explanations. "Those are possibilities, yeah."

Colin's head moved in the barest shake. "It's not just that." His gaze fixed on the floor, but Grace heard the certainty in his voice like a shiver up her spine.

Will sighed, long and weighted. "If a kid's involved, this isn't a game. If we screw this up, it's not creaky pipes and wasted hours. It's a boy. We're not professionals. If something goes wrong, it's on us."

The silence that followed was different this time. Not

comfortable. Heavy.

Julian cracked it with a grin too bright for the mood. "Well. At least if we all get horribly cursed, Theo'll have company."

Will shot him a glare hard enough to pin him to the wall.

"This isn't a joke, Jules," Colin said, stern in a way that silenced the room. He shoved his untouched bowl into Will's hands as he stood. A moment later, his bedroom door slammed, rattling the frames on the wall.

Julian winced, mouth half-open. "Something I said?"

Grace exhaled shakily, forcing herself not to look at the door. "It was a long time ago," she said. Her fingers dug into the denim at her knees, nails biting half-moons into the fabric. "There was a boy in our eighth grade class who came back from the summer break different. He was lethargic, not speaking up, and falling asleep during lessons. Honestly, someone should've caught it sooner. A teacher should have intervened, but it was Colin who noticed."

"He called it a shadow presence," Will said, voice clipped.

Grace nodded, throat tight. "He was sure it was clinging to the kid, making him sick. This boy had been a straight-A student, involved in everything. And then suddenly it was like he was empty. He was barely holding on to a C-average. Colin said he could feel a dark presence attached to him. He asked for my help. He wanted to reach out to the other kid and I knew him better."

Julian leaned forward now, curiosity stripping the smugness from his face. "And did you?"

Grace's breath snagged. Shame seared through her, the same sick churn of sitting across from Colin on her bed and telling him what she thought was the 'sensible' answer. "I told him to let the school handle it. That it wasn't a good idea to get involved. Colin was already picked on at school and I didn't think it'd go over well. Two weeks later the kid was found dead in his bedroom."

The room went still.

"Jesus," Lance said, wrapping his arms around her waist from behind like he could keep her together by sheer force.

"They said it was natural causes," Will said grimly, not meeting anyone's eyes. "They said he just stopped breathing in his sleep."

Grace pressed the heels of her hands to her eyes, blinking hard, but the tears slipped free. "Colin's never forgiven himself for not stepping in," she said. "I doubt he's forgiven me either." Silence hung over the group as even Julian, usually quick with some irreverent quip, was staring down at his hands as if the story had pinned him there.

Will's jaw flexed; his silence was the loudest thing in the room.

"Will—" Grace started, her voice soft but unwavering and desperate. "We can't walk past this one. Not again. It'll kill Colin to turn his back."

For a beat, Will held his ground. Grace saw the urge in his frame, the desire to pack everything up, shut down the team, wrap Colin into blankets and keep him away from the darkness. He must've known as much as Grace that Colin would never back down. He exhaled slowly, as if he were giving up ground he hadn't realized he was standing on.

"Fine," he said at last. His voice was quiet, but it cut through the stillness. "But we do this carefully. My way. No cutting corners."

The tension broke in a rush. Grace closed her eyes, shoulders sagging with relief. She hoped they wouldn't already be too late.

CHAPTER 3

JULIAN

Julian had never been good at leaving things alone, least of all Colin Vale.

He could still remember the first time he saw him, nearly a decade ago now. Colin had been a scrawny little thing then, all long limbs and angles, ears he hadn't quite grown into, and moving with the loose, loping gait of a colt still figuring out what to do with its legs. He was beautiful and shy, with a laughter that came late but landed like sunlight through a crack in a boarded window. It was almost impossible not to look at him.

Julian had only been two years older, sweating behind the fryer at the diner down the street, under Will's management. He still wasn't sure why Will had chosen him out of the mess of sullen teenagers orbiting that place. It couldn't have been his charm. He had next to none back then. He was fresh off his father's sudden abandonment, clocking hours at a job he hated just to keep the lights on at home, juggling three younger siblings, and a chip the size of a boulder on his shoulder. He wasn't anyone's first draft pick for friend material.

Will hadn't asked about any of that, though. As far as Julian was aware, Will didn't even know. Somehow though, he saw past the skinny kid slinging burgers like it was punishment and, one night after catching him bumming cigarettes in the alley, brought him home.

And that's where Colin had been. Sitting on the arm of their thrift-store sofa, hair too long, watching Julian like he was equal parts curiosity and annoyance. Julian's whole bad-boy act did not impress him. The first time he knocked back a shot without blinking, Colin just raised one unimpressed eyebrow, like he'd seen tougher in the mirror that morning.

That was the thing about Colin: he never gave Julian the satisfaction of playing along. He didn't swoon at Julian's dramatics or scold his sharp tongue. He watched, patient and steady, like he was waiting to see what would happen once Julian ran out of tricks. Maybe that was why Julian had stuck around.

The years hadn't dulled that pull. If anything, they'd honed it into a bone-deep awareness of Colin Vale and the way his silences spoke louder than words. He didn't need to say much to make Julian feel seen and, infuriatingly, stripped bare.

The very first kiss was enough for Julian to know they'd never make it. It was late, one of those marathon horror movie nights where the bad acting became its own entertainment. Will had passed out on the couch behind them, sprawled and snoring. Colin was eighteen then, all bright eyes and crooked smiles, looking cherubic in the blue glow of the screen as he picked apart plot holes with giddy precision. Julian hadn't planned it. One second he was watching Colin's lips move, cataloguing every shape of amusement, and the next he was leaning in, reckless, pressing his own mouth against them.

They lasted less than a month. Not a flame, but a supernova, gone before anyone could blink but brilliant while it burned. Julian had never stopped thinking of it as both the worst and best mistake he'd ever made. He still loved Colin, but he also knew, with the same clarity he'd had in that first kiss, that Colin would never love him back.

Now, in the same cramped apartment, Julian waited for the others to wrap themselves up in their plans before he slipped away from the noise and made his way to Colin's door. The room was dim, curtains drawn against the city lights. Colin lay curled on top of the covers, his long frame folded in on itself, hoodie sleeves tugged down over his hands like he could hide inside them.

Something twisted in Julian's chest. He'd seen a handful of nights like this, when Colin would disappear into himself as everything became too much. All Julian could do was sit nearby and hope his presence was enough. He crossed the room quietly, listening to Colin breathe and willing himself not to reach out.

"Col, we don't have to take this case if it makes you this worried."

For a long moment, Colin didn't move. Julian thought maybe he'd drifted off, but then he saw the flutter of his eyelids, the way his jaw clenched like he was holding something back.

"You don't get it," Colin said finally, voice muffled into the pillow.

Julian leaned back on his hands, trying for casual even as his chest tightened. "Then make me get it. I know I'm slow, but I can be trained."

Colin huffed a bitter laugh. "That remains to be seen." He

sighed. "It's nothing."

"Bullshit." Julian angled himself so he could see his face. "I saw the way you froze up the second Lance said 'Ashford.' Don't lie, Col, not to me."

Colin curled tighter, like he was trying to disappear into himself, then he exhaled, long and shaky, and turned his head toward the ceiling.

"I've been dreaming about them," he said. His voice was barely above a whisper, but the words cut clean through the quiet.

Julian's pulse stumbled. "Dreaming—about the Ashfords?"

Colin nodded. "I think they're warnings. I see the house and the name, Ashford, written in blood. A lion with a snake for a tail. I've been dreaming about it for weeks, and every time I wake up, it's like...like something's trying to shove me toward it." His hand curled in the fabric of his sleeve, white-knuckled. "I didn't want to say anything. I thought if I ignored it, maybe it would stop. But the minute he said Ashford..."

Julian's throat went dry. Colin didn't spook easily, not in basements, not in graveyards, not in the dead of night. His whole life had been a living nightmare.

"You should've told us," Julian said. "You know, Will—"

"That's why I didn't." Colin's eyes flicked toward him, raw and wary. "If the house wants me there, then I'm already in it, and if I can help this kid so he doesn't end up like me one day—"

"Hey now," Julian chided. "I quite like you just as you are."

Colin smiled. "I know. Still, I have to try, Jules."

Julian nodded. He knew Colin well enough not to bother arguing. "I'll watch out for you, I promise," he said. Colin didn't answer. His eyes fluttered shut, and whether he was asleep or only pretending, Julian couldn't tell. He stayed anyway, staring into the dark, until the muffled sounds of the others in the living room blurred into nothing but background noise.

The Ashfords were waiting, and Julian had the sick sense that whatever Colin had seen in his dreams was already breathing down their necks.

CHAPTER 4

LANCE

Lance had always been most solid when everything else teetered. He moved through chaos like a ship cutting through storm-tossed waves—steady, unshakable, his senses alert while everyone else flailed. His four-year stint in the Navy had honed that instinct into something almost automatic. In the middle of a disaster, Lance's mind ran like clockwork, breaking down problems into clear, measured steps. He couldn't afford to panic when someone else depended on him.

Tonight, that calm was a quiet companion rather than a necessity. He and Grace moved through the narrow streets, the occasional streetlamp casting puddles of gold across wet asphalt, their shoulders brushing as they navigated uneven sidewalks. Lance reached over to lace their fingers together, a subtle anchor against the residual tension from their planning session. Only three blocks separated them from their new home. Grace had insisted on staying close to the Vale's and Lance was willing to fold on just about all of her requirements as long as he got to keep this.

They had moved fast, some friends had warned, but Lance didn't believe in slow dances with destiny. The new apartment was two stories and larger than either of them were used to, so it was a slow process to settle in. Boxes leaned like weary soldiers against the walls, still taped shut, their labels half-legible. Stacks of mismatched dishes teetered precariously by the sink. The front rooms were still missing curtains and Lance had put a throw blanket up as a temporary fix. To Lance, it already felt like home: warm, lived-in, and just a little chaotic in the best possible way.

He glanced at Grace as they approached the door, the soft curve of her cheek catching the glow from the flickering streetlight. Her hair had fallen loose from the ponytail she'd tried to tame all day, a few strands brushing her temple. A familiar certainty settled in his chest. This was right.

"Think we should unpack a box tonight, or let it wait for a lazy Sunday?" he asked as he swung open their door. The warm air from inside rushed out to meet the evening chill.

Grace laughed softly, the sound bouncing off the walls of the narrow hallway. "Let it wait," she said, stepping inside. "We'll survive the clutter one more night."

Lance stepped in behind her, inhaling the mixed scents of cardboard, paper, and paint. They shed their coats and shoes in the narrow entryway, the soft thud of leather boots against the hardwood echoing faintly. Lance let himself relax against the door for a moment, arms crossed, watching Grace move through the apartment like she belonged in every corner already.

The kitchen light flickered on, pale and warm, and Grace busied herself at the sink, rinsing off a coffee mug to make herself tea.

For a moment he just watched, taking in the beauty of her. He kept mulling over what Arthur had said to him that morning before speaking with Grace, *I always took you for too level-headed to believe in ghosts.* At the time, he'd laughed it off, told Arthur that he was playing along because it was important to Grace, but now that he thought about it again he had to admit that he was less than convinced.

"Do you really think there's something going on with Arthur's nephew?"

Grace glanced over her shoulder, arching an eyebrow, a smirk tugging at her lips. "You mean, do I believe the boy is in danger? Or do I think the supernatural is real?"

"Both," Lance said, shrugging. "I mean, our last three cases with your friends have all been drafts, plumbing, and raccoons. I guess I expected more theatrics when you told me what you all do."

Grace let out a soft sigh. "Honestly, I'm glad for the cases where nothing happens." She paused, watching Lance raise an eyebrow. "I know you're a secret adreneline junkie. I see how much you love the rush of danger, but I've seen plenty of things go badly. I don't need that every time."

Lance smirked, leaning against the counter opposite her. "I like to consider it 'good in a critical situation,'" he said, teasing, though there was a note of seriousness under the words.

Grace chuckled, shaking her head. "Sure. But it's not just about you or me." She set the towel down and folded her hands over the counter, gaze drifting to the cluttered piles of papers and boxes scattered around the apartment. "You know," she said, voice softening, "I didn't always believe in Colin, either."

Lance tilted his head, curiosity flickering. "Oh?"

"Yeah." Grace leaned back, pressing her palms to the counter. "I humored him because he was weird. And because I was his only friend. A kid with that much imagination, that much sensitivity? It could've crushed him if no one cared." Her lips pressed together briefly, a shadow of memory crossing her face. "But ten years in, seeing him grow into this person who feels everything. I've seen things I can't explain. *Impossible* things. And it's only a fraction of what Colin encounters every day of his life. Can you imagine? The bravery it takes to survive that and then have nobody even believe in you?"

Lance's expression softened. He walked over and took her hand, fingers threading with hers, the simple warmth a tether against the quiet unease that lingered from the evening. "I get it," he murmured. "I don't need to see a ghost to respect that. You've watched him, and you trust him."

Grace nodded, squeezing his hand. "Exactly. And maybe I don't need to see ghosts, either. I just need to know that when things get heavy, we're in it together. With him and with each other."

Lance's lips curved into a gentle, reassuring smile. "Then I guess that's enough for me."

She leaned her forehead against his shoulder, letting the hum of the apartment settle around them. Outside, the streetlamps glimmered across the wet pavement, and inside, amidst the clutter and chaos, Grace and Lance let themselves simply be.

CHAPTER 5

COLIN

The van's tires crunched over loose gravel as they turned onto the long, winding drive of the Ashford Estate. Before the house came into sight, Colin felt it prickling at his consciousness, the tiniest of warnings that made his skin itch. It wasn't fear exactly, but a tremor under the surface, like a heartbeat echoing through stone.

He tried to focus on the obvious things first. The house itself loomed on a slight rise, sprawling and formidable, cloaked in ivy that strangled the stonework. From this distance, it was magnificent in the way old wealth always was: vast, commanding, untouchable. The obvious signs of neglect betrayed the beauty. Many windows either had cracks or were boarded shut. The stone had faded unevenly, streaked with moss and black water stains, and the roof sagged over the westernmost wing, the corners curling as if the years themselves had grown weary of holding it up.

The grounds were no better. The lawns, which were once sculpted with manicured precision, had become wild and rebellious. Long grass waved like a storm-swept ocean, weeds tangled with the remnants of flowerbeds, and statues stood chipped and twisted from the hard touch of sun over the years.

Colin's hands rested on his knees, fingers flexing almost unconsciously. The estate radiated something he couldn't name: anger, yes, but also something darker. It didn't breathe, and yet it had a pulse, faint beneath the surface.

From the back, Julian's voice carried: "Christ, this is basically a castle! If we kick out the ghosts, you reckon they'll let me rent a room permanently?"

Lance scoffed. "Julian, they'd pay you to leave."

"True," Will agreed, smirking. "You couch-surfed for three days, and I nearly murdered you."

Grace let out a bright, melodious laugh at that. "Will, you nearly murder most people daily."

Peripherally, Colin listened to his friend's banter, but his attention was on something less tangible: the currents beneath, the invisible lines that whispered of what the house had seen.

The driveway opened onto a circular courtyard. Colin noted the fountain: a cracked lion head gaping open, tongue of stone missing, silent and accusing. The residue of centuries settled into the cracks of the space, lingering, as if the estate's memories were clinging desperately to the last shreds of its grandeur.

Lance, sitting beside Grace, fidgeted. "Does anyone else get the feeling someone's watching us?"

Colin didn't answer. He didn't need to. The estate's attention brushed over them, skimming the edges, pressing against the edges of awareness. Lance was right; it was watching. Waiting.

Measuring.

Grace sighed. "Silent houses hide secrets," she said, almost to herself. Colin heard the caution in her voice, faint, like a ripple in water. He turned to her, noting the tension around her jaw, and knew they were both remembering a different child, years ago, trapped in a haunted house and tortured by it. Houses like this left impressions on children. They were raw conduits for things that waited unseen for the wrong moment.

Will leaned back in the driver's seat, muttering about "rats in the attic" and "faulty plumbing," and Colin allowed himself the smallest, almost imperceptible shake of his head. It was comforting in a way, the predictability of Will's annoyance. But it didn't touch the unease at the edge of the property.

"Stay close," he said, more to himself than anyone else, as he pushed his way from their vehicle, trusting the others to follow.

The large oak front door opened before Colin knocked, and the woman who appeared was like a storm held in human form. Her dark hair curled at her temples and hung well past her waist, with a few strands stubbornly clinging to her sweat-damp forehead. She had a face that belonged in forgotten oil paintings, pale as moonlight, with cheekbones carved to catch candlelight. Her eyes, a glacial green flecked with gold, held the bearing of royalty, and despite her weary face, there was a command in her stance.

"Can I help you?" Her voice was tight and defensive, though not unkind.

Colin gave the faintest nod. "We—uh, we're the ghost hunters?" The lady arched a fine eyebrow at his timidity, and Colin cursed himself inwardly for the misstep. This was not a time to fall prey to a beautiful woman. "I'm Colin Vale. This is Grace Lovette." He waved Grace forward as the point of contact.

"We spoke on the phone briefly last week. Arthur requested we come," she said.

Something thawed in the woman, her shoulders dropping in release, and she gave a rueful smile. "Right," she nodded. "He told me you were coming. I thought you wouldn't be here until Friday."

"It is Friday," Julian said, tactful as ever. Colin resisted the urge to scowl at him and smiled as he heard the telltale thwap-squeal of one of the crew walloping him in the head for his trouble.

"If you need to reschedule," Colin began.

"No, no," the woman said, near frantic, cutting off his retreat. "Sorry, no. I must have lost track of the week..." she paused for a moment, deep in thought, then shook herself free of it. "Anyway, please come in. I'm Alexandra, by the way. Everyone calls me Alex."

"Colin," he said again, then stepped into the tiled foyer. "This is the team — Grace, Lance, Julian, and Will. We all have our specialties, but we work together to do a thorough investigation, including ruling out everyday sorts of things that can sometimes feel supernatural."

"What sorts of things feel supernatural but aren't?" a small voice asked. Colin turned, surprised to find a compact figure crouched under the receiving table. The boy was dark-skinned and wiry, all angles and dark, watchful eyes. The flesh beneath them was dark with bruises from stress or lack of sleep. Colin caught the subtle rhythm of his movements, the way he didn't fidget but was never still either.

"Lots of things," he told the child, crouching down to join him under the furniture. "Electric problems, old pipes. Last week a family called us in to check out their haunted attic," he joked, rolling up his sleeve to show the four long lines of a healing scratch. "Turned out to be a family of raccoons."

The boy's eyes grew large, and he gave a soft huff of laughter. "I'm Theo," he said after a beat.

"Hi Theo," he greeted. "I'm here to help."

"Can you?"

Colin looked over the rest of his team in quick assessment. Julian leaned casually, all charm and amusement, sizing up the place and calculating the number of cameras he'd be setting up. Lance hovered at Grace's side, hands shoved into his jacket pockets, steady and stalwart and ready, as always, for anything. Will tightened his jaw and scanned the shadows with his eyes as if predators lurked there instead of peeling paint. And of course, Colin was already aware of things they hadn't seen yet. "We are going to do our best," he offered.

The sound of crisp footsteps echoed across the hall before anyone could speak again, heralding a tall, imposing man in slacks and a neat button-front shirt. He was tall and broad-shouldered, and moved with the calm confidence of someone born to money and influence. His hair, sun-kissed and golden, fell in an artful tousle to his temples and framed a face that was equal parts mischief and steel: a strong jaw, a mouth quick to smirk, and eyes the color of a summer sky on the verge of thunder.

Colin couldn't help but wonder what was in the Ashford gene pool to have produced two perfect humans, such opposites in appearance but somehow both the most beautiful people he'd ever seen.

"I see the Ghostbusters have arrived," he said dryly, in lieu of an actual greeting. It immediately made him 20 percent less attractive, or so Colin told himself. He quickly surveyed the room, stopping at Colin, who realized he was still tucked under the table with Theo like a child himself.

He grimaced and rose to his feet, brushing off his trouser legs a bit sheepishly. "I'm Colin," he said, holding out a hand to shake.

The man's eyes narrowed, and he didn't accept it. "Arthur," he said, "will you need a crystal ball for this, or just the fee upfront?"

Colin suppressed a snarl, though his mouth twitched with the sarcasm that had long been his defense mechanism. "No crystal ball needed," he said, tone light but edged with irony. "A human sacrifice is sometimes necessary, though. Are you volunteering?"

Arthur arched an eyebrow at the insolence, evaluating, undecided whether Colin was competent, insolent, or both. Colin's pulse quickened, not with fear, but with the same subtle jolt he always got around people who challenged him. He hated to admit it, even to himself, but Arthur had a presence. And presence was magnetic.

Behind him, Lance stepped up and began the introductions of the remaining team to smooth out the heaviness that now hung in the surrounding room. When Arthur was busy, Grace stepped up to Colin's side and nudged him with her elbow. "Careful," she said. "He's already on edge, and the boy needs us here."

Colin glanced over his shoulder at the child. Theo's eyes were still on him with the same unsettling intensity as before. The boy's gaze didn't flicker or look away. It was steady, unnervingly perceptive, as if he saw beyond what Colin allowed others to see. Colin's stomach tightened.

"Perhaps we could sit down somewhere and you can explain what's been going on here," Colin said, directing his attention back to Arthur.

Arthur gave a noncommittal grunt, then turned on his heel without another word, expecting—assuming—they'd follow.

Alexandra rolled her eyes behind his back with theatrical exaggeration and gestured for the group to come in.

They followed Arthur through a long, dim hallway lined with faded portraits that judged their pass with cold, indifferent eyes. The floorboards creaked beneath their feet, and the air was dusty with something old and metallic. Colin swore the house contracted around them, like lungs holding breath.

The drawing room was cavernous and cold despite the late summer heat outside. One of the tall windows was open, allowing in a thin stream of pale light that failed to chase off the shadows. The furniture looked antique and uncomfortable, draped in protective linen, like the house had gone into mourning. A fire had been lit recently, the logs still crackling in the grate, though it did little to warm the room.

Arthur took up a stance near the mantel, arms crossed. He wasn't lounging; he was bracing. His entire posture screamed reluctant host, or maybe warden. Alexandra perched on a faded armchair and reached for a chipped porcelain teacup, as if they were merely here for a social call.

"It started with the clocks," she said. "They kept starting and stopping. The chimes would go off at all hours of the day and night."

"And then the doors started opening," Arthur said, voice clipped. "No wind, no drafts. Just swinging open. Slamming shut. Waking the whole damn house at night."

"It escalated quickly," Alexandra continued. "Theo started sleepwalking. Always trying to get into one of the locked rooms."

At that, Will straightened. "What room?"

"The study," she said. "It was my father's. We haven't been inside it since we took over the property a month ago. I don't have the key."

A long silence followed that.

Colin leaned forward, brow furrowed in thought. "Have you called in a locksmith?"

Arthur shook his head. "Not yet."

"In truth, we weren't particularly eager to get into the room," Alexandra said. "We've heard noises too, sometimes from behind the study door, sometimes footsteps pacing through the halls. They...they try the bedroom doors, so we have to keep them locked."

Something cold settled at the base of Colin's spine.

"It's a full job," he told his team, catching their eyes one by one. "Overnight. Wire everything."

"I'm sorry," Arthur scoffed. "Did you just invite yourselves to stay in our home?"

"You invited us, actually," Colin smirked. "You don't need to trouble yourselves. We brought sleeping bags and can make up a base camp in any unused space."

Arthur scowled, likely ready to argue further, but Alexandra swept in with false cheer. "This place could use the company, anyway. Let me make up some guest rooms for you all."

"Really, that's not necessary," Grace simpered.

"I insist."

"Well then, I insist you let me help," Grace smiled. The two women left in a flurry of chatter and movement, and Colin tried very hard to be mature and not preen at winning one against Arthur Ashford.

For his part, Arthur didn't reply, but a muscle in his jaw flexed. A protective instinct, Colin noted, not of the heroic, warm kind, but of the grim, weary sort. Like he'd been keeping the world out by sheer force of will for too long, and the cracks were showing.

As the team broke off into their roles and began setting up the base camp, Colin lingered by the hearth, gazing into the fire, halfway between thoughtful and haunted.

The house was watching, listening, and it was not pleased to have them here.

CHAPTER 6

ARTHUR

The light outside was fading, and with it the house exhaled into something darker. Shadows stretched long across the floor, pooling like ink. Arthur had grown up in these oppressive halls. The place was different without staff bustling through the corridors or fires burning in the hearths, stripped of polish and pride, but its bones were the same. He still knew where the floorboards creaked near the grand staircase and that the third door on the left in the east wing never shut properly. The smell hadn't changed either: faint wood polish dulled by dust, and something colder underneath.

He'd never thought of it as home. August Ashford had made sure of that. His father filled every room with authority and left no space for warmth, and Arthur had spent his boyhood learning how not to flinch under that assessing gaze. Even now, with ivy pressing at the windows and mold climbing the ceiling, it felt as though August might stride in at any moment to find fault with him. The house remembered, and it judged, just as August had.

Arthur stood with his arms folded at the threshold of the sitting room, watching the so-called "investigators" spread out like they owned the place. Strangers' footsteps echoed off rooms that hadn't heard laughter in years. Already the air was alive with their voices and with the low hum of electronics. It was invasive, like weeds forcing through paving stones.

The only familiar face belonged to Lance. Arthur had met him through his law firm last year when Lance's non-profit had been looking for a lawyer to give legal advice to unhoused LGBTQ teens. They'd struck up a genial friendship. Lance was the sort of man who made people reevaluate what they thought charm meant: dark eyes, an honest smile, aristocratic cheekbones and a sense of compassion that made saints seem selfish. At least Lance moved with purpose, bent over the table in the sitting room to arrange neat coils of cable beside blinking monitors. His competence was reassuring.

Will was, all together, less careful. He muttered to himself as he scattered little packets and lengths of string across the room, a man preparing a siege in someone else's fortress. There was a restlessness in him, a coltish strain of tension that was never far from breaking into motion. He wasn't classically handsome, but there was warmth in his honey-colored eyes and in the boyish cut of his face despite being a few years Arthur's senior. Arthur's brows drew down as Will began pouring a thin white line of something across the perimeter of the sitting room.

"What are you doing?" he asked, sharper than he meant.

Will looked up, defiance already in his eyes, but he only shrugged. "Most spirits won't cross a salt line."

Arthur scoffed. Superstitions, charms, gadgets. It was all

absurd. And yet, he didn't tell him to stop.

The worst offender, though, was the shaggy-haired one. Julian. He was broad-shouldered, rangy, and rough-hewn, like someone had carved him from sturdy oak and left him out in the rain to weather artfully. His hair curled into his face no matter how often he pushed it back, and somehow that only added to the impression that rules were for other people. He worked with a careless cheer, hauling wires over his shoulder, crouching to tape equipment in place, and whistling tunelessly down the estate's corridors. The sound carried eerily.

Arthur pinched the bridge of his nose. It was absurd, all of it. But as the last smear of daylight drained from the windows, the old prickle returned at the back of his neck.

Ashford walls watched. And remembered.

He shook himself. Refusing to give in to the flights of fancy that had tortured him throughout his childhood.

"Do you always take over someone else's home like you own it?" he asked at last, his voice cutting across the room's busy chatter.

Heads turned. Colin's was the last. He was crouched by one of Julian's monitors, his dark fringe hiding his eyes until he looked up. Arthur had an unwelcome and irritating sense of being seen too clearly.

Colin gave a faint smile, the kind that made it seem like Arthur had told a joke. "Would you rather we knock on every door first? Ask the ghosts nicely where we can plug things in?"

Grace stifled a laugh; Lance hid a smile.

Arthur narrowed his eyes. "I'd rather you didn't treat this place like a playground."

"Playground?" Colin stood, brushing his palms against his

jeans. "Trust me, Ashford, no one here thinks of this place as fun."

Arthur bristled at his surname in Colin's mouth, too formal and reminding him of his father. "Then why are you here?"

Colin's reply was simple. "Because you asked us."

Arthur scowled at being caught out. It was infuriating. *Colin* was infuriating, with his dark hair, and bright eyes, and slender build, and full, smirking lips. The idea of a grown man making a living by hunting ghosts was so absurd that it made the parts of Arthur who had strived and toiled every day for an ounce of acceptance and pride, bristle. Worse still, Colin was completely indifferent to Arthur's sour mood.

Arthur exhaled, conceding without words. Grace was already taking notes, Will was finishing his little circles of salt, and Julian had vanished down some corridor muttering about "hot spots."

Only Colin stayed still, anchored at the center of the chaos. His face was all rigid planes and pale angles, so that he looked almost unreal, like he'd stepped out of some fantasy novel about elfin creatures. Those stormy-blue eyes pinned Arthur with a clarity that scraped uncomfortably near the bone. He was like a contradiction wrapped in skin: fragile yet stubborn, gentle yet fierce.

Arthur hated that he couldn't seem to look away.

Julian's voice cut through the moment, loud and intrusive, bouncing off the high ceilings. "Uh, Col? We've got a situation."

Colin snatched the walkie from a nearby chair, the plastic creaking under his tense fingers. "What kind of situation?"

"The kind where my cameras are losing their minds," Julian replied, tinny and distorted. "Every time I put one up in the east hallway, it glitches and goes to static. Three units so far. The tech's fine. I triple-checked the wiring."

The team froze, eyes widening as if the air itself had thickened. Then, almost in unison, they darted toward the door. He followed reluctantly, curiosity gnawing at him, a faint thrill curling along with the fear.

When they arrived, Julian, perched precariously atop a creaking ladder, legs braced against the rungs, was swearing a symphony of colorful words at the tiny black handheld he gripped. "It's the damndest thing," he said, climbing down and handing the device to Colin. "Only been recording for five minutes, but look."

He flicked open the view window, and the group leaned in. At first, the hallway looked ordinary: faded wallpaper, worn floorboards, two doors opposite each other. Then, just before the feed glitched, a ripple of something shimmering, shadowy, and indefinable slid across the screen. Static followed, loud and sudden.

"Well, it's obvious, isn't it?" Will scoffed, arms folded. "Julian put his fat fingers on the lens."

"Hey! First of all, these are precision-engineered hands," Julian shot back, wiggling them like a master flaunting his craft. "Practically art. Besides, I was packing up when this happened."

Arthur observed as the group orbited Colin and deferred to him. Colin's eyes had grown distant, unfocused, as if something unseen tugged at the edges of his perception. He stared down the hallway, which dead-ended in another door.

"Enough of that," he whispered.

"Enough of what?"

Colin blinked, as if surprised to find Arthur there the whole time. "Um… nothing," he hedged in a way that obviously meant *something*. "What do these doors lead to?" Colin asked after a long pause.

Arthur turned, taking in the hallway with fresh eyes, and an eye-roll threatened at the predictability. "Alex," he said, pointing to the left door. "Theo," he said to the right.

Colin's nod was almost imperceptible, as if he'd expected the answer. Arthur wondered what he'd picked up on to pull off that particular con. He'd seen that before on those mentalist debunking videos. They gave silent clues to indicate important places and people. He resolved to be more wary going forward about what information they shared. Alex might want these nuts here, but he was not in the mood to be conned by a beanstalk who claimed to talk to ghosts.

"We should put some wards up," Colin said, "at least around Theo's door. Just in case."

Arthur crossed his arms, lips pressed into a tight line. "Fine," he said, voice tight with exasperation. "Come on, ghost-hunter. Let's see what you've got."

Colin rolled his eyes, and Arthur bristled at the effortless dismissal. "Hold your horses," Colin chided, retrieving a piece of chalk from a pocket—as if it was a perfectly normal thing to be carried around at all times—and knelt on the floor, drawing intricate shapes on the wood in front of Theo's bedroom.

"That's oak, you know," Arthur said, more to have something to say than from genuine concern for the furnishings and trappings of the withering house.

"I'll be sure to wash it before I leave," Colin said with a smirk. Arthur tried not to notice the soft vibrations in his voice, how the words settled in the air, and how Colin's eyes kept darting past him. A chill crawled along the back of his neck, the faintest thrill of being watched.

Colin finished, eyes lifting to meet Arthur's for just a heartbeat too long. Arthur wanted to look away, mutter some snide remark about theatrics, but he nodded.

"Done," Colin said, stepping back. "Should help keep it out, at least tonight." He moved on to check the other doors. Arthur's gaze followed, against his will, before he quickly tore it away, pretending to focus on anything else.

CHAPTER 7

LANCE

The house breathed differently at night, heavier and deeper, like a resting beast.

The monitors' glow painted Lance's face pale blue. Only the hum of electronics accompanied him. One screen tracked the staircase, another the west hall, another fixed outside Theo's door. The boy hadn't stirred since his mother tucked him in hours ago.

Everyone had peeled away one by one, claiming exhaustion or the need to "regroup." He doubted anyone was actually getting sound sleep, but he was happy enough to volunteer for the night watch.

He was still finding his role on the team, but he could do this much: sit steady in the silence, keep his eyes on the monitors, and keep watch. He enjoyed being useful.

The building was old enough to groan and settle like a restless sleeper, each creak in the rafters pulling his attention. He told himself it was just timber adjusting against the press of wind through the night. But the longer he sat, the heavier the air grew, until the house leaned in close.

A flicker in the corner of one monitor caught his eye. At first, he thought it was a trick of the light or a shadow shifting with the house. But then he saw it: a figure approaching behind him, reflected in the screen. Grace.

Relief warmed him like a small sun. His shoulders, tense from hours of sitting, loosened without thought. "Shouldn't you be asleep?" he asked. "Or are you checking up on me?"

He didn't look back immediately, letting himself drink in the reflection for a moment: her curly hair falling loose, the soft line of her jaw, the easy tilt of her head. He loved that about her. Grace didn't need to try, didn't need to perform. Every little gesture made her luminous, like she carried light without realizing it.

Lance swallowed, his lungs tight with the strange, familiar ache of admiration. How had someone as boring, as predictable, as him earned her time or affection? It was beyond him.

The reflection in the monitor shifted closer, and Lance exhaled, a small, appreciative smile tugging at his lips as he felt the heat from her body behind him. "You shouldn't be up," he said again, this time letting the gratitude and relief slide into his tone. "I don't mind keeping the watch all night, really."

She smiled, or at least he thought she did. The angle made it hard to tell. He leaned back into her, savoring her touch as her hand moved to his shoulder and squeezed comfortingly.

"Well, I won't turn down a quick neck rub," he joked, leaning into the hand and letting the tension in his shoulders ease further. Hours upright staring at screens weren't great for his posture, and he groaned as she began kneading at the knots along his scapula with practiced precision. "Oh," he breathed, "that's the spot. I really needed that."

He thought he heard her hum in acknowledgement, but her fingers began pressing harder, digging under the knots and into the sensitive spaces below, unyielding.

"Ouch." He dropped his head to pull his body away from her ministrations. "I'm a wimp, Grace, you know you can't massage me that hard," he teased to soften the rejection of her comfort. Her hands didn't stop though, only gripped tighter so that the blunt edges of her nails bit into his skin with bright bursts of pain.

"Grace—hey, that's—stop, that hurts," he gasped, twisting to shrug off the hand. He spun around, heart hammering, ready to meet her eyes with reproach or concern.

Only, there was no one there.

The room was empty.

Lance pressed his hand against his shoulder, wincing as the throbbing beneath his fingers radiated down his arm. His pulse hammered in his throat, quick and uneven, each beat echoing in the room's stillness.

He glanced back at the monitors. Nothing. Every hallway frozen in the same sterile glow, the staircase empty, Theo's door silent. The cameras captured no movement, no hint of anyone lurking nearby.

Lance drew in a slow, deliberate breath, forcing himself to focus. He adjusted his chair so he could see the doorway this time, spine rigid, every nerve tuned to the faintest shift of shadow.

Then he heard footsteps, soft and careful.

The door eased open, and Grace stepped inside, her silhouette caught in the dim light behind her.

Lance's throat grew tight. His first thought was, *not again*. His second was worse: *what if it's her this time?*

"You're still up?" She asked, keeping her voice lowered so as not to wake anyone.

He didn't answer right away. His eyes flicked between her face and the monitor, half-expecting the reflection to betray her. But the screen showed the woman he loved: soft curls, loose sweater, gentle smile.

"Lance?"

"Don't—" he said harshly, and she froze where she was. He dragged in a breath, palms slick with sweat. "Don't touch me. Just…give me a second."

Grace frowned, worry knitting her brows, but she obeyed, raising her hands. "Okay. You're scaring me a little."

"Good," he said, then winced. "No—not good. I just—Grace, I thought you were here. A minute ago. I *felt* you." His hand went to his shoulder, rubbing hard against the throbbing ache. "You put your hand on me. I swear to God, I thought it was you. Until it wasn't."

Her face went ashen. She stepped slowly closer, like he was a skittish animal she didn't want to spook. "It mimicked me?"

"Yeah." The word came out hoarse. He gave a short, ugly laugh. "Fuck, it touched me!" When he reached for her, his hands were trembling. "That is—"

"First ghost sightings have that effect." Grace moved to his side, eyes focused on where he gripped his shoulder. "Let me see."

He hesitated, then turned for her to lift the hem of his shirt. Her fingers were warm and steady against his neck, a shocking contrast to the phantom chill that lingered in his skin.

Grace sucked in a breath. "Oh, Lance…"

"What?" His voice jumped.

"There's a mark. Like fingernails. It broke the skin." She

brushed her fingers there, and he hissed when her touch grazed the raw edge. "You're bleeding."

For a moment, neither of them spoke. The silence pressed thick, broken only by the faint hum of the monitors.

Finally, Lance said, quieter, "Then it wasn't in my head."

Grace met his eyes with an ironic smile. "No. You *were* hoping for more adventure this time."

He swallowed hard. "I've never even heard of something like that. I didn't know they could look like people you know or...or touch you."

Grace let out a soft laugh, nodding. "Sometimes places really are haunted. People too. And it can get dangerous."

"I'm getting that," Lance said. Grace's hand lingered at his back, not quite touching the wound, but near enough for her steadiness to radiate through him.

"We'll tell the others in the morning," she said. "For now, I'll stay awake with you so it doesn't get another chance."

He wanted to protest and tell her he could handle it, but the truth sat too heavy. He nodded.

The monitors hummed on, their pale glow flickering against both their faces. Grace pulled a chair beside his, folding herself small in the seat, curls falling over her shoulder as she studied the screens with him.

For a few breaths, the silence was almost normal again. Almost.

Then, on the far left feed, the west hall camera stuttered, static chewing across the frame before it cleared.

The hall was empty.

He blinked hard, pulse jumping. When he glanced to his left, the real Grace was still there beside him, keen-eyed and very real.

"You okay?" she asked.

Lance hesitated, then shook his head. "Not even close."

The house creaked above them, as though in agreement.

CHAPTER 8

GRACE

Grace followed the narrow hall out of the sitting room, the lingering tension from watching monitors all night still knotting her spine. Lance's shoulder was stiff under her hand, but he seemed steadier now, breathing slow and even. She let the adrenaline of the night ebb, though her thoughts refused to stop replaying the image of that phantom touch.

The Ashford kitchen smelled like vanilla and eggs, a comforting contrast to the chill that clung to the rest of the house. Arthur was already there, sleeves rolled up, hair sticking out at odd angles, surrounded by an alarming spread of frying pans and bowls. Bacon sizzled in one pan, pancakes puffed in another, and eggs glimmered under the yellow kitchen light. Flour dusted the counters like powdered snow. Grace paused, a small smile tugging at her lips.

"Arthur," she said, stepping inside. "This is kind but unnecessary. We usually just get McDonald's."

Arthur turned, eyes wide and his face disgusted. "McDonald's? Look, I know your resident psychic would call it snobbery, but we will not be bringing McDonald's into this house."

Lance followed, rubbing his shoulder absently, and Grace noticed the tension still lingering in his posture despite the calm of the kitchen. "I didn't know you could cook," he said, easing the prickliness radiating off their host. "You should do a class at the shelter for the kids moving into state residences."

Arthur's gaze flicked between them, like he was trying to decide if he was being made fun of. Finally, he released a breath of tension and shrugged. "Cooking is soothing."

Grace moved over to the eat-in dining table at the far end of the room and plopped down into a cushy, if dusty, seat and let the warmth of the kitchen soak into her. "I get that. Sometimes it helps to channel all your energy somewhere tangible."

The creak in the hall drew their attention just as Arthur was stacking the first pancakes onto a plate. Will entered, hair slightly mussed, shirt messily buttoned and half tucked into his jeans, and a faint scowl that didn't quite reach his eyes. He glanced at the cluttered counters before he began shoveling food onto his plate with a kind of happy, unquestioning efficiency that made Grace suppress a laugh. Bacon in one hand, eggs in the other, he navigated the kitchen like a man who had survived too many late-nights to care about appearances.

Grace's eyes met Lance's across the table, and for a long moment the only sound was the sizzling of bacon and the clatter of utensils.

"Okay," he said, voice low but firm, "I need to tell you about last night. Something happened."

Arthur froze mid-flip of a pancake, spatula suspended in

midair. Will froze mid-bite, eyes narrowing slightly as he looked at Lance with scrutiny. Grace's pulse ticked up a notch, her fingers tightening around her chair.

"What kind of something?" Will asked cautiously.

Lance exhaled, steadying himself. "I saw someone. Or some*thing*. It looked like Grace. It touched me."

Will blinked, and for a second Grace thought he might not believe him, but there was something about Lance's calm, measured delivery. He was a man who calculated risks, who had stared down storms and bullets, speaking with unshakable certainty.

Arthur's brow furrowed, flour smudging the side of his face. "Touched you? Like…physically?"

"Yeah," Lance said, nodding once. "Fingernails, pressure, even drew a little blood. It was real, and I didn't imagine it." He turned slightly in his chair, pulling aside the neck of his shirt to show the crescent-shaped marks where the thing's nails had dug into his flesh.

Will's fork hovered mid-air. "Haven't had a full manifestation in a while," he said, turning to Grace with a raised eyebrow.

Grace nodded. "We knew this one felt different from the beginning."

Arthur made a sound somewhere between a scoff and a snort, waving a hand at Lance's back as if brushing them off could erase the story entirely. "I don't know," he muttered, scratching the back of his head. "Maybe you just scratched yourself in your sleep during a weird dream? It looks a bit like cat scratches. We had a cat when we were younger. It ran away, but it could definitely still be on the property—"

"You think I confused a cat for my girlfriend?"

Arthur didn't answer for a long moment. "I think a lot of things are more likely than ghosts," he said.

Will leaned back in his chair, arms crossed, eyes narrowing as he considered Lance's words. "We shouldn't tell Colin yet," he said finally, voice low but authoritative. "He's already on edge, and this... this will throw him further. He'll feel responsible."

Grace nodded, relief washing over her that Will was thinking about Colin's state of mind. "Agreed," she nodded. "He doesn't need more weight on his shoulders right now."

Lance exhaled, a brief release of breath. "Yeah, okay," he said, brushing a hand over the raw skin on his shoulder, trying not to wince. "I'll keep it between us for now. But we need to stay alert. This...thing doesn't care about whether Colin's ready."

CHAPTER 9

COLIN

The smell hit him before anything else — rich, buttery, and overwhelming. Colin blinked against the early sunlight filtering through the guest room's dingy windows, his stomach rolling uneasily. He was already queasy, a familiar side effect of too much exposure to paranormal forces. The onset had been more abrupt than usual, but the sensation wasn't altogether uncommon.

When he'd been fourteen, the lady down the hall from them had died in her apartment and then stuck around and haunted him. It had been a terrible month of flu-like symptoms, bloody noses, and almost no appetite before he could help her move on.

He lingered in bed as long as he dared, willing the waves of nausea to ebb, before dragging himself upright and pulling on a clean pair of jeans, a soft tee, and a thick sweater to guard against the estate's chill. Following the scent of breakfast, he moved down the narrow staircase and along a corridor, each step deliberate as he fought the dizzying lurches in his stomach. When he reached the kitchen, the scene that met him was almost domestic in its perfection.

Arthur, despite his usual prickliness, appeared to have arranged a substantial breakfast: eggs piled high, bacon curling in neat strips, toast stacked like tiny towers, and a steaming pot of coffee sending curls of vapor into the morning light. Diced fruit waited in a crystal bowl that gleamed on the table.

Most of the team had already gathered, eating and chatting. Grace's laughter drifted through the room, bright and soft, while Will rumbled something that made Lance snort. Julian, of course, was absent and likely buried deep in sleep. Colin knew from experience that it would take a stern word and a well-placed thump to rouse him before he was ready.

He paused at the doorway, gripping the frame and swallowing hard to ground himself before moving toward the open seat at the eat-in table. The frequency of this house was something he'd never experienced before, like being scrutinized by a disapproving father. Every misstep, every act of defiance came at a cost in this home, leaving no room for humanity or warmth. He reveled in the moment, between the hiss of the frying pan and the indistinct murmur of conversation, where the oppression loosened.

Arthur moved around the stove with unexpected ease, flipping the final pancake onto a heaping stack and turning off the hob. Colin expected to order breakfast, but Arthur's calm, unhurried movements showed competence and a practiced hand in the kitchen.

Colin watched more closely than necessary, noting the calm strength in Arthur's movements, the way his sleeves rolled just so, the faint crease of focus between his brows. There was something magnetic about the way he handled the simple act of cooking: controlled, deliberate, undeniably capable. Colin's chest tightened, a mix of admiration and frustration he didn't want to acknowledge. Part of him wanted to lean in, ask questions he had no business asking, prod at Arthur's careful barriers to see if he could get a reaction. It was maddening. Every instinct told him to stay as far from this man as possible, but it also yearned to test the limits.

Arthur carried the last stack of pancakes to the table, adding it to the feast already laid out.

"You're not eating," he asked, furrowing his brow at Colin's empty plate. He scooped it up and began piling on eggs, toast, and fruit. "Did you need an adult to help you fix a plate?"

The team reacted as a whole: Grace snorting into her coffee, Lance shaking his head with a bemused grin, and Will letting out a truly raucous guffaw.

Colin scowled. "I am perfectly capable," he snapped, accepting the plate Arthur held out to him without thinking. The smell made him want to throw up, so he took a deep breath and swallowed. "I just—I never really eat when we are on a case," he said when Arthur would not move out of his space or his business without an explanation.

Arthur raised an eyebrow, skepticism etched in every line of his face. "Well, that can't be healthy."

"It's… a paranormal side effect: nausea and headaches."

"And nosebleeds," added Will, unhelpfully.

Colin scowled. "Sometimes I just can't eat when we're in a place like this." Colin shrugged self-consciously.

Arthur's frown deepened. "Paranormal, huh?" he murmured, dubious. Colin nodded, feeling heat creep into his cheeks. He'd never had to explain his eating habits to a client before.

Arthur exhaled, muttering under his breath, but relenting. He turned on his heel, dropping the plate on the counter, and moved toward the fridge. A moment later, he returned with a white-labeled bottle and placed it before Colin, smirking. "Lucky for you, I always keep a protein shake on hand for busy mornings."

Colin took it, letting the minor act of care ground him. The warmth of the kitchen and the murmured teasing was just enough to ease the shadows pressing at his thoughts, and he forced himself to take slow sips of the sweet, milky drink.

Loud footsteps coming from the hallway shattered the quiet conversation and heralded Julian's arrival.

He barreled into the kitchen like a hurricane, hair tousled, jacket half-zipped, and made a beeline for the coffeepot, like it was a homing beacon. He poured a tall mug of black coffee and turned to face the others, beaming with his usual wild abrasiveness, and Colin braced himself.

"Morning, everyone!" Julian said, voice bouncing off the high ceilings and offering a devilish smirk. "You will not believe the dream I had last night. There was this blonde babe—"

Colin groaned inwardly, already dreading the details. He opened his mouth to intervene, but Julian continued, motioning suggestively, "—and she was stacked like a—"

Colin's hand shot down to the table, pressing hard against its edge. His cheeks flamed. "Julian. Now is not the time," he hissed, jerking his head toward the doorway to remind him they were in a client's home.

Julian froze mid-gesture, blinked at Colin, and then shrugged as if nothing had happened. "Ah, right. Spoilsport," he said, though that mischievous glint never left his eyes.

A soft shuffle of shoes on polished floorboards announced another arrival moments later. Colin's senses prickled at the recognition. He'd sensed Theo moving nearer, an unsettling and new sensation. He'd never been around another person like himself before, and it felt sort of like having a radio in his head tuned to another person's frequency. Alexandra appeared in the doorway with the boy tucked at her side, clutching a book and staring at the assembled crew.

Arthur straightened, tilting his head. "Morning."

Julian, now aware of the child in the room, blinked and threw his hands up. "Ah! Morning, little one!" he said, lowering his voice dramatically, though Colin caught the faintest trace of embarrassment behind the grin.

Colin rolled his eyes, regaining control of the room. "Right. Let's get a plan for today," he said, voice firm but measured. "Will, can you do a perimeter sweep? Check for bad plumbing, wiring, gas leaks, the usual." Will nodded, stretching his shoulders like a coiled spring, already moving into position.

"Julian, you're in the control room. Watch the monitors and, for God-sake, radio me if you see something; don't wander off to chase a ghost." Colin teased, a smirk tugging at his lips as Julian gave a dismissive "Pfft," and took another large gulp of coffee.

"Grace, you are, of course, on research," he continued, and Grace nodded, pulling her laptop from her bag.

"And what will you be doing?" Arthur asked him, with something like a challenge in his voice.

"Preparing for a séance. I want to see if we can lure something out."

"Something?" Alexandra asked, her voice thick with worry.

Not something, Colin knew. *Someone.* He had been catching

him in the corner of his eye since they'd entered the estate yesterday afternoon: a cold, tall figure lingering in every shadow. Knowing it opened a veritable quagmire, Colin turned to face the woman and asked, "Tell me about your father? This was his home before your inheritance?"

All the air sucked out of the room with the simultaneous gasps from the Ashford siblings. "Why do you need to know?" Arthur asked.

Colin bit his lip, aiming to tread carefully. "There's a presence here. Imposing. Angry. He's everywhere and infinite but strongest in the shadows. I need to know who I'm dealing with before I summon him."

Arthur scoffed, equal parts incredulous and angry, but it was Alexandra who answered. "You couldn't have described my father more accurately," she admitted. She glanced over at her brother, standing at the kitchen counter, tense-backed and glaring. She seemed to ask him a silent question, but whatever answer Arthur gave her was unclear to Colin.

"Okay," she said eventually. "The thing you have to understand is that August raised us to believe that to be an Ashford was to be perfect," she said with a sardonic smirk. "Some of us embraced the notion like a seed planted and watered," she motioned to her brother. Then she indicated herself. "Some of us were always meant to be weeds."

"You and he didn't get along," Colin surmised.

Alexandra laughed. "It's a bit more complicated than that. For a while, I was his pride and joy. He doted on me, spoiled me rotten, really. I got good grades, prestigious awards, was well-liked in his high society groups—then I met a boy." Here she rolled her eyes, and Colin could hear Arthur huff an angry growl from his periphery. "I got pregnant at seventeen," Alexandra said, resting a gentle hand on Theo's shoulder. She turned to him and smiled sweetly. "I hadn't planned it, but I was still excited, of course."

He kicked you out?"

Alexandra smiled and nodded. "He said he disowned me, though apparently he never made that legal in the paperwork since I inherited the house." She shrugged. "It was hard and scary for a few years. The boy I loved was monstrous, and we separated before Theo was even born. I worked shitty jobs and lived in shitty apartments, and I did my best."

Colin could almost see it, a younger Alexandra Ashford, stubborn and strong and unyielding against her father's old-school mentality. Each of her acts of rebellion would feel to him like an erasure of his name, a dent in the monument he had spent decades building. He had tried to shape her in his image, not out of love necessarily, but because he measured his worth in authority over his family.

Colin turned to face Arthur, who looked caught out, his face tight and stricken. For a moment, he thought the story would end there and Arthur would not deign to tear down his barriers for their sake. After a long breath, Arthur said, "The day I turned eighteen, I came out to my father." He grimaced at the memory. "He took it about as badly as I had expected him to. If you can believe it, the thing he was angriest about was not having an 'heir' as though we were 16th century royalty. He kicked me out too, with a single backpack of clothes and a cellphone that he disconnected service to." An ache settled into his chest at the confession. "I tracked down Alex, and she helped me. I got into an excellent school, took night shifts and worked odd jobs —construction or whatever I could get—to pay the bills until I passed the Bar. We both washed our hands of August and his Ashford pride. For six years we were completely free of him."

"And then I got word from a lawyer that I had inherited the estate."

"We didn't even know he was sick," Arthur said.

Colin sighed. It was both what he expected and somehow worse. "The thing about houses," he said after a moment, "is that they absorb energy."

Arthur scoffed again, but Colin didn't give him space to protest. "This house was the place where August Ashford walked empty halls steeped in his own rage and misguided pride. The house has become an extension of him in that way. He's seeped into the foundation here. He hides in the shadows because the house has been empty, but eventually, the longer me and Theo are here, the stronger he'll get and the more trouble he'll be able to cause."

"Theo," Alexandra asked, startled.

Colin nodded apologetically. "I sensed it in him when we met yesterday." He turned to face the child. Theo frowned but gave a nod himself. "All children are sensitive to the paranormal," Colin said. "Some just notice it on the fringes. They're less influenced by the world, less wary of the supernatural forces around them. But sometimes, a child is so keyed into the energy of a space, they can cross the boundaries. It's scary, isn't it? Seeing things nobody else can see?"

Theo shivered but offered a small nod again. "He's always right behind me," he said.

"I know. Me too."

"Alright, that's quite enough," Arthur barked, his face livid and red with his anger. "You can play your games in the estate and even for Alexandra, but you leave my nephew out of it. He is *ten*;

he is highly susceptible to influence, and your parlor tricks will confuse him."

"You don't have to believe in me," Colin conceded, "but you called us here. I'm giving you an answer. Take it or leave it."

"What can we do?" Alexandra interrupted.

Colin grimaced. "Like I said, a séance to draw him out is my first step. I need to communicate with August, figure out why he's lingering here and what he wants."

"Besides being a bigoted dick," Julian grumbled.

Colin huffed a tired laugh. "Right. If we can figure out what he's after, we can help him move on. Usually, even the angriest spirits don't want to be trapped here anymore than you want them hanging around."

"The study," Alexandra said, turning to Grace. "You're researching the estate and the family? It'll be in my father's study. I don't have a key, but it's the best place for us to start."

"Excellent," Grace nodded, packing up her laptop and rising. "Can you show me there?"

"Yes, but how will you get in?"

Julian jumped up enthusiastically. "Oh, leave that to me. I've never met a door I couldn't crack," he smirked.

"I am not surprised," Arthur huffed, still irritable.

The ladies, followed by an ebullient Julian, quickly packed away their breakfasts and headed back out into the house on a mission. The motion was enough to break the thick tension that had taken over the room, and everyone jumped up at once to attend to their various tasks. Eventually, only Colin and Arthur remained in the kitchen, the latter glaring at the former.

Colin lingered by the counter, watching Arthur's profile as he sorted through the remnants of the food. The tension in the room had thinned, but a new, quieter unease settled around them.

"I'm trying to understand why you called us here when you don't want to believe this place is haunted?" His voice was careful, but there was an edge of genuine frustration that he couldn't quite contain.

Arthur straightened, jaw tight, eyes steady on Colin. For a long moment he said nothing, and Colin wondered if he'd answer at all. Then, slowly, the edge in his posture softened. "There's very little I wouldn't do for my sister and my nephew," Arthur admitted, his voice firm, carrying a burden that made Colin pause. "Even if it means swallowing my doubts and letting 'specialists' handle what I can't see for myself."

Colin blinked, taken aback by the simplicity of the truth and the unwavering sense of responsibility Arthur carried.

He nodded once, letting the words settle and the lingering heaviness in the house ease. For the first time that morning, he allowed himself a small, resilient hope: perhaps, together, they could face whatever shadows lingered here.

As he thought it, a chill brushed across his skin, subtle but insistent, bringing the faint, unmistakable touch of a presence: patient, watchful, and very much still the master of the house.

CHAPTER 10

WILL

Will's boots crunched along the gravel driveway, the sound too loud in the thin morning. The Ashford estate sprawled around him like a slumbering giant, the brickwork softened by moss, shutters cocked at odd angles, and gutters clogged with the detritus of several neglected seasons. From the road it might read as a handsome ruin; up close it read as a house that forgot itself. To Will, it read as a checklist.

He walked the perimeter with his hands shoved into the pockets of his worn corduroy jacket, eyes taking everything in with economical precision. Most "hauntings" had mundane causes: bad plumbing, warped floorboards, loose wiring, and he planned to find them before anyone lit a candle or called a spirit. The sooner they could satisfy the Ashford family's fear, the sooner they could get Colin out of here. He knew he couldn't ignore the ominous atmosphere in the place, especially after seeing the look in Colin's eyes when they arrived, but he owed them a proper investigation.

The west wing's brick finish looked almost like a weathered map of faces, cracks yawning into shapes that, in the wrong light, seemed to leer. Will ran a finger along the mortar, feeling for hollow spots, tracing a hairline fracture like a surveyor. Decades without repointing had let frost and rain pry at the joints. He pulled a folded notepad from his pocket and sketched a quick map of the property, marking an X where the mortar flaked worst. If a draft funneled through there, it could easily set a door slamming at an inopportune moment.

A crow startled from the gutter with a hoarse caw, wings beating the air in ragged strokes. It flew low across the lawn and disappeared into the bare arms of the oaks. Will looked after it for a beat, annoyed, then moved on.

The east façade fared only marginally better. An old line of oaks crowding the property edge had protected the masonry from the elements, but their roots were pressing up through the foundation like impatient hands. He tugged a root up by the wall and frowned down at the smear of black mildew where moisture pooled beneath the sill. Mold could explain a lot of things: headaches, dizziness, paranoia. He jotted another note, his handwriting tight and professional, though part of him admitted a single-week of exposure seemed unlikely to explain the severity of the symptoms the Ashfords were experiencing.

Condensation fogged the glass of a first-floor window, and when he rapped a knuckle against the frame, the pane rattled loose in its setting. On stormy nights, the whistling wind could sound like someone whispering in the hall. He squatted to probe the seal with his fingers and felt the breath of a draft. Another box checked.

The back garden had turned half-wilderness, brambles and skeletal roses lacing the air with damp soil and rot. Branches scraped at clapboard; weeds threaded under the window wells. He pulled a thorny stem free and brushed dirt from his gloves. A few scratches on a pane, and an overactive imagination—or a frightened child—could swear they'd seen hands press at the glass.

Will catalogued and rationalized: faulty masonry, drafts, mildew, rattling panes, a garden gone feral. Logical, fixable, if someone with a ladder and money cared to tend to them. Still, there was a heaviness that pressed into his sternum if he stood still too long, as though the house itself were stealing his breath. That was harder to ignore or explain away. Will straightened, rolling his shoulders back to break the sensation.

He climbed the porch steps, each board complaining under his boots with an ominous groan. The ornate front door loomed ahead, unnaturally tall with scabbed paint and a tarnished brass handle dulled to a weary brown. Will reached out, intending to test the hinges, when it creaked inward on its own.

He paused, nonplussed. The wind did not blow at his back, and the door did not swing as if hung incorrectly. The opening was slow and deliberate, as though the house had been waiting to welcome him back in.

Will froze, hand suspended midair. His reflection stared back from the dusty glass inset, faint and warped. For a long breath, he simply stood there, pulse thudding, every instinct yelling that he should not step over that threshold.

Then his rational brain caught up. Wind. Draft. Settling foundation. All explanations he could catalog and test. He stepped forward and shut the door firmly. The latch clicked into place.

He pulled at the handle. Solid. He jiggled it again. No give.

"Right," he muttered, jaw tight. He opened it deliberately, swung it wide, then let it fall shut. This time it thudded into place without complaint. He tested it again, tugging and slamming until the brass rattled in its setting. Nothing unusual.

Kneeling, he inspected the locking mechanism, running his finger along the strike plate, checking for wear. Everything looked normal. No cracks in the wood. No loose screws.

Still, he tried it again. Shut. Tug. Open. Shut. Tug. Nothing.

Will straightened and rubbed his palm against his thigh, as though brushing away the moment. But the feeling clung like a cobweb across his face. He glanced back at the long drive, at the overgrown garden beyond. Empty.

"You're losing it, Will."

But when he turned back, the door, shut and latched only seconds before, hung an inch ajar, as if mocking him. Will's breath hitched. The door hung just wide enough for a person to slip through, the shadowed seam of the entry yawning at him. He swore under his breath and pushed it shut again, harder than necessary, the thud echoing through the foyer.

Will exhaled, forcing his shoulders to relax. Later, he could check the jamb. He could explain this. He *would* explain this.

Then his walkie-talkie crackled to life on his hip, sudden and startling, and he jumped as he fumbled at his pocket to pull it free.

"Will," Julian's voice said over the static, brisk and urgent, "get to the office. Now."

The words snapped through him like a wire pulled taut. "What's going on?" he asked, already moving back through the door, leaving it to shiver against its hinges in his wake.

"It's Colin," Julian replied.

CHAPTER 11

ALEX

Her father's study was dusty, and the air was stale in a way that made Alex's stomach twist. Sunlight fought through the narrow windows, catching motes of dust in its beams, but the light did little to dispel the heaviness. It felt wrong, thick, as though the house had absorbed decades of anger and disappointment, then exhaled it into the air.

Julian had broken into the space with alarming ease and an online lock-pick kit. He'd offered a wolfish grin after letting her and Grace into the room and saluted before heading back to the sitting room to watch the cameras.

Theo lingered near the doorway, body tense, as she and Grace entered. She kept one eye on him as they inspected the space, noting the way he tracked shadows that didn't move and corners that held nothing.

Colin had arrived a bit after, seeming to sense the door was open before anyone radioed to tell him. He creased his brow in discomfort as he moved around the room, pressing his hands outwards like a mime trapped behind an invisible wall, and he walked the perimeter with intense concentration. When he reached the spot behind the desk, where her father's imposing wing-backed chair waited, he visibly flinched and stepped away.

"He's in here," Colin said definitively.

A chill ran up her spine at the thought, and she could almost conjure the image of her father's imposing figure in that seat, glaring down at her in disapproval and judgement.

Sure and methodical, Colin began placing a line of equipment across the front edge of the mahogany desk: a voice recorder; a handheld device, roughly the size of a thick smartphone, with a matte black casing and clear glass screen; an unlit candle; and a temperature gauge.

Colin adjusted the items with deliberate care, and his gaze flicked to Theo, who had inched closer to be at Colin's side. Their eyes met for a fraction of a second; no words passed, but the connection was tangible. Alex's worry eased. Despite Arthur's misgivings about this whole thing, she was grateful they'd called Colin and his team. Something was already settling in Theo.

He had always been a quiet child, a habit born of a hard upbringing, but since moving into the manor, his silence had grown stiff and frightening. He had once confided in her, trusted her with his secrets, yet over the last month she had watched him turn completely in on himself. Watching him interact with Colin, she realized how stark the difference had become and how Colin's steadiness was coaxing her son back out.

One by one, they flipped through the devices together. Sometimes using them to scan the room, sometimes asking questions of the space and waiting for a response. After almost an hour of diligently working through the tools to no avail, Colin let out a frustrated groan. "Nothing," he scowled angrily. "He is right fucking there, and he isn't answering," Colin huffed, turning furious eyes to the still empty chair.

Alex looked at Theo, but the boy had not taken his eyes off the chair in question for several minutes and was now slowly backing his way towards the door, biting his lip.

Grace moved a little closer, but Alex kept her distance. She didn't want to crowd Colin when the air was already heavy and suffocating. The stillness was almost worse than activity. It meant that whatever presence they were dealing with didn't want to be reached, which begged the question: why was it here?

Alex shifted from foot to foot, keeping herself near Theo, eyes darting between Colin's movements and the shadowed corners of the room. She couldn't see the presence he might sense, but she knew it was pressing in all the same.

"Alright, August," Colin said, his whole body sagging with the defeat. "Your way it is." Without warning, he circled the large desk and pulled out the chair.

Grace called out for him to stop, but before she could step forward, Colin had dropped into the seat with a soft thud. Alex held her breath, watching. Almost immediately, something changed. His posture stiffened, and his fingers gripped the arms as if he were bracing for impact.

His eyes darted rapidly, flicking in every direction as though he were scanning a thousand details all at once. Alex could see it in the way his jaw tightened, the way he sucked in a shallow breath. She couldn't tell what he was seeing, but it was enough to make the hairs on her arms stand on end.

Theo shuffled all the way into her side, his sneakers scuffing against the rug. He reached out with his smaller hand and clutched at the hem of her blouse, knuckles pale against the deep burgundy fabric, like a child bracing against a storm.

"Colin?" Grace asked. He didn't answer. His lips moved, breath shaping almost inaudible murmurs. The chair creaked beneath him as if the wood itself strained to contain him. The sound crawled up Alex's spine. He wasn't just sitting there, suspended in some invisible current that held him rigid. His eyes darted beneath his lids in rapid, unnatural flickers, like someone flipping too fast through reels of film.

"Colin," Grace said again, sharper now. She gripped his shoulder, fingers pressing into the fabric of his jacket. "Hey! Colin!" She shook him once, twice, the motion jerking him in the chair. He didn't stir. The mutters spilling from his lips only deepened, strung together in syllables that sounded fragmented.

Her stomach twisted, a knot of fear winding tighter with every breath. The study was small, airless, as though the heavy books and shadows leaned in to listen.

"Alex," Grace said, her tone clipped but urgent, "I need you to go find the others. Will or Julian, okay? Go. Now."

Alexandra's body obeyed before her mind caught up. She bolted from the room, the old floorboards protesting with groans under her feet. Her heart was in her throat, and she nearly collided with Julian. He was in the hall, muttering at one of his cameras, the device braced in his hands.

"Damn thing," he said, then he looked up. The moment his eyes landed on her, his expression shifted. He read the panic that showed on her face. The camera dropped to his side with a dull thud, and he strode toward her.

"What's going on?"

"It's Colin," she gasped. "He's in a trance or something. In the study."

Julian's frown hardened into something heavier, more serious than she'd ever seen from him. Without hesitation, he pivoted toward the east wing, already fishing his walkie from his belt.

"Will," his voice snapped over the static, brisk and urgent, "get to the office. Now."

A beat later, Will's voice crackled through, wary: "What's going on?"

"It's Colin," Julian replied.

CHAPTER 12

JULIAN

J ulian had been in a lot of strange rooms, but this one was different. Ashford's study had a stale, metallic taste that made every breath feel like sucking air through an aluminum straw. The heavy curtains and dirty windows let only slivers of light in, thin bands of gold that slanted across the desk and bookcases. Dust motes drifted through those beams like ash, clinging to the leather spines and gleaming wood panels, but nothing about the light softened the atmosphere. If anything, it exposed it. It was like sitting in the lungs of something old and mean, waiting for it to exhale.

Colin sat rigidly in the oversized chair. He looked more statue than man, jaw clenched, lips moving in broken whispers, fingers locked around the chair's arms as if welded there. His eyes jittered beneath their lids, frantic and unnatural, like reels of film spinning too fast for the projector.

Will crouched in front of him, his hand braced on Colin's knee, the other hovering in hesitation over his brother's arm. His voice was low and coaxing. "Colin? Col, it's me. You're okay. I'm right here, alright? Are you with me?"

Colin continued muttering raw, mangled syllables that stretched thin. The sound crawled under his skin, raising gooseflesh along his arms. He busied his hands, because if he didn't, he'd start panicking. The tripod clicked into place beneath his grip, each lock snapping loudly in the silence. He mounted the camera with deliberate care, then lined up the EMF reader. Next came a voice recorder. Each piece slotted into the routine like muscle memory, steady precision to combat the gnawing unease. He forced himself not to look too long at Colin.

Across the room, Lance mirrored him. The other man's face was pale, jaw tight, but his hands didn't falter. He adjusted lenses, tightened screws, and flicked switches with brisk efficiency until the study thrummed with their equipment: a ghost-hunter's chorus, all quiet hums and blinking red lights.

Julian pointedly avoided Alexandra and her boy. The moment they'd entered, Theo had fled to his mother's side and hadn't moved since. He clung to her blouse like a lifeline, small fingers white-knuckled in the fabric. He fixed his dark eyes unblinking on Colin, as if he was watching a nightmare he already knew the ending to.

Arthur was the last to arrive. Julian wasn't even sure how he knew to join them here. He said nothing, folding his arms across his chest and leaning back against the shelves with suspicious eyes and a scowl.

The room bent itself around Colin in his strange trance. The muffled air pressed in thick, swallowing their movements, their voices, even their breaths. Julian's own pulse sounded too loud. He adjusted the camera display and pretended to check its focus, but the feeling gnawed at him, the prickling certainty that something in the dark corners was watching them back.

He cleared his throat; the sound jarring in the hush and called out just loud enough for Will to hear. "Equipment's ready, boss."

Will lifted his head, gave a curt nod, and rose from his crouch. His eyes lingered on Colin's face before he turned away, exhaling through his nose like a man bracing for impact.

"Right," he sighed. "I'm going to bring him out by calling the spirit free." His gaze snapped to Alexandra and Theo in warning. "If you don't want to be here for this, I recommend leaving now."

The woman understood at once. She tugged gently at her son's arm, whispering something urgent, but Theo only shook his head once, emphatically, 'no.' His stare never broke from Colin. Alexandra tried again, voice pleading now, but the boy's refusal was iron. At last, she relented, slumping against the door with Theo still clinging to her like a limpet, his small body tense and unyielding.

Will nodded his understanding and straightened, his voice cutting clean through the stillness. "I'm speaking to the spirit that has my brother in thrall," he declared, firm. "We wish to communicate with you."

For a long, trembling moment, the only reply was silence. Then, the room shifted.

A whisper slithered through the air, warped and hollow, like wind rattling through a broken pipe. It crawled along the walls, garbled but deliberate in its cadence. The sound made Julian's gut clench.

Colin gasped suddenly, sucking in air like a drowning man breaking the surface. Then his head snapped back, and he wailed, the sound jagged and inhuman, splitting the air like a knife.

"Release him!" Will shouted, his voice booming with a fury Julian had never heard from him. "If you wish to communicate, do so!"

The scream cut off abruptly. Colin sagged forward, shoulders slack, his body folding into itself like a puppet with its strings cut.

The lights flickered once, twice, then exploded. Bulbs burst in a strobing cascade, glass raining to the carpet as a violent flash plunged the room into darkness. The only light left was a single candle sputtering on the desk, its flame twitching erratically.

Julian's heart lurched as movement drew his eye. Theo's knees gave way, and he fell to the ground next to his mother as if he were a marionette and someone had cut his strings. His slight frame curled tight, convulsing. Alexandra lunged to gather him, panic written across every line of her face, but his trembling made it impossible to hold him steady.

"Stop!" Colin's voice cracked through the chaos, hoarse and loud, yanking every eye toward him. At once, Theo stilled, the convulsions dying into shivers. He trembled, but from fear and exhaustion now, not some unseen grip.

Colin was standing free of the chair. He braced his hands on the desk and breathed raggedly.

"August Ashford," he rasped, his voice commanding, "I release you from this sacred circle." He leaned forward and blew out the candle, plunging the room into temporary darkness.

The wail that followed was ear-splitting and ripped through the study, rattling the glass panes, and then there was silence, heavy and absolute.

Julian fumbled at his hip, fingers closing around his flashlight. He snapped it on; the beam cutting through the gloom as Will and

Grace mirrored him, their lights scattering the darkness. With a blink, sunlight reappeared through the curtains, thin but real, as though someone had pulled it back into place.

Alexandra sagged to her knees, dragging Theo into her arms, his breaths heaving fast but steady now.

The study held still, heavy, but the air carried the stench of ruin, like smoke after a fire, something scorched and unfinished.

Colin swiped sweat from his brow, slumping with exhaustion. His eyes scanned the room once before he said wearily, "That was unexpected."

Arthur was on him in seconds, fury written across every line of his face. "What the hell were you thinking?" he snapped, storming forward. "You sat in his *chair*?" Arthur's words came out ragged. "What even was that?"

Colin blinked at him, hollow-eyed, and for a moment Julian thought he might laugh at the question. "I think it was your father."

Arthur's expression twisted, disbelief etched in every hard line of it. "My *father* is dead! Do you even hear yourself?" He dragged a hand through his hair, pacing a short, angry line across the rug before stopping short again, eyes fixed on Colin. "Christ, this was such a stupid—"

He cut himself off, jaw clenching. Julian saw a flash of something beneath the fury. Fear. Arthur's fists kept opening and closing, as though holding himself back from shaking sense into Colin or pulling him out of harm's way; he couldn't decide which.

Colin didn't answer. He looked back at Arthur with a strange, stubborn weariness. "You called us here," he said. "What did you expect would happen when we investigated ghosts in your home, Arthur?"

Arthur scoffed, incredulous. "I expected you'd pull a few parlour tricks with a deck of tarot cards and leave."

Will bristled at the implication, but Colin let out a tired puff of laughter. "Happy to rise above your expectations," he smirked. He moved around the desk on weary legs but refused his brother's help when he rushed to Colin's side. "I'm fine," he said in assurance, patting Will's shoulder and pushing himself more upright, "Just gotta get out of this room for a bit. Theo should rest."

Arthur gave some sort of grumbled response, but turned to his sister and nephew, scooping the child up into his arms easily and heading out of the room as well.

When the last of their footsteps faded, everyone left in the study exhaled. Julian stood with his hands braced on the camera, knuckles white, trying to ground himself in the metal and plastic. Across the room, Grace rubbed her temples, eyes distant, while Lance busied himself with packing up the recording equipment.

Julian let out a laugh that was humorless to his own ears. "Well," he said, "if that was the welcoming committee, I can't wait to see what the house saves for dessert."

Grace lowered her hand and glanced toward the door Arthur had left through. "I've never seen Colin do anything like that," she said warily. "Even at his most tapped in, he's never been in a trance like that."

"Do you think he'll be okay?" Lance asked.

Grace bit her lip. "He always recovers."

"Eventually," Julian added with a frown. The machines blinked their red lights back at them, steady and indifferent. His gaze drifted, unwilling, to the wing-backed chair. The leather looked dull in the fractured daylight, lifeless again, just a piece of furniture. But the memory of Colin in it, mouth moving, eyes rolling, the house bending in around him, clung like smoke.

Julian adjusted the camera once more, though it didn't need it, and tried not to think about the way the candle's last hiss had sounded almost like laughter.

CHAPTER 13

ARTHUR

Arthur held his breath until the corridor swallowed the study behind him. Colin's ragged command still echoed in his mind. Stop. As if it were simple. As if a man could sit in his father's chair, invite the house's darkness in, and then dismiss it like a servant.

The nerve of it made Arthur's jaw ache from clenching. Fury burned hot and immediate, but beneath it, unwelcome and stubborn, was something far worse: fear. He hated its lingering, hated that he'd imagined pulling Colin out, tearing him away before the house swallowed him whole. He couldn't explain the pull he felt towards the strange man.

Forcing his thoughts back to reality, he shifted Theo in his arms. The boy's weight was light but solid and warm against Arthur, steadying him. Alex walked at his side, silent, her hand brushing Theo's back from time to time, as if to remind herself he was still there. She hadn't said a word since the fit had passed.

Neither had he.

Silence suited him. Words were harder to trust when his thoughts tangled with rage and dread, disbelief stitched tight with something like concern. He kept walking, jaw tight, each step carrying him further from the study, though not far enough to leave Colin's reckless face behind. He still couldn't believe it, couldn't fathom what possessed Colin to sit there willingly, at the epicenter of danger. The thought twisted like a knife: a deliberate offering, a risk he had no authority to veto.

An old ache followed, the gnawing frustration of powerlessness that had haunted him since childhood. There was a part of him that had always needed to protect, always needed control. Alex called it his "hero complex," and he knew it rankled her, but it wasn't about pride or masculinity. They'd grown up in a prison of expectations and shadows. Everything in his body screamed at him to keep others from such a fate.

"Arthur?" Alex's voice pulled him back. The worry in her eyes mirrored his own, but beneath it lay trust, a reliance he couldn't ignore. He gave a curt nod, more to steady himself than to acknowledge her.

Theo stirred against him. "I want Colin," the boy said, voice small and uncertain.

Arthur's breath caught. *Me too*, he thought, then wanted to throttle himself for it. "After you get some rest," he said.

Theo shook his head, insistent but ultimately powerless. "But I gotta tell 'im somefing." The boy's words slurred in his fatigue.

"Whatever you need to say, we can tell him later," Alex said, guiding them toward the bedroom. Theo huffed, grumbling, but surrendered to exhaustion.

Arthur pushed open the door to the boy's room, stepping over the drawn sigils Colin had chalked on the floor yesterday.

"This was a bad idea," he said as he laid his nephew into the four-poster bed, tucking him in. "I shouldn't have brought them here. Lance is usually so level-headed, but everything is just getting worse."

"Are you serious? Thank *God* they're here, Arthur. Do you think we could handle this on our own?"

Arthur grimaced. "Handle *what*, Alex? So far we've had some bad feelings and a sleepwalking kid. Before they came, nothing dangerous had even *happened*. This is all theater to scare us and con some money?"

His sister's nostrils flared, fury simmering, but she said nothing further, brushing a kiss over Theo's hair before beckoning him into the hall like he was a misbehaving child. "After everything you've seen, all we've witnessed today, you aren't seriously going to keep acting like this is all in our minds, are you?"

Arthur stiffened, jaw tight. He wanted to assert authority, to lean on reason and caution, to remind her that logic was the only shield he had, but the memory of Colin in that chair, of Theo screaming and convulsing, undermined his every conviction.

"Arthur," Alex said softer now, probing. "I know you have always been reasonable. I know that's who August raised you to be. But sometimes things are out of our control. Some things are beyond reason. It's okay to trust Colin, even if the thought terrifies you. Maybe what you're really afraid of is connecting with someone who isn't me or Theo. You know that, don't you? It's okay if you feel something for him."

Arthur's throat closed. He opened his mouth to deny it, to reject it outright, but the lie stuck. "Don't be absurd," he said halfheartedly, gaze snapping to the floor. His fists clenched.

She didn't push further. Instead, she gave him one last assessing look. "Think about it," she said. "Sometimes the hardest things to face aren't the demons in the house; they're the ones inside ourselves."

Arthur remained by the door, pressing his back against the wall, eyes forward, and let the silence stretch. The manor was heavy around him, ordinary again on the surface, but the thought of Colin still pulled at something inside him.

Arthur had spent his whole life navigating the legacy of August Ashford. At first, it was hero worship. Then obedience. Then disillusionment. And finally, a bone-deep fear that no matter how far he ran, no matter how different he tried to be, he'd turn into him, anyway.

He trembled at the thought. He drew a steadying breath, jaw tight, and huffed again. The estate groaned as if in response, timbers sighing, ancient pipes clanking. Light pressed against the windows but couldn't penetrate the space with brightness or warmth. Arthur shifted, trying to shake the unease, but the boards beneath his boots creaked like they were warning him to stay still.

He didn't notice Colin until the man was already halfway down the corridor, his steps soft but certain. Exhaustion bruised the skin beneath Colin's eyes, making him look drawn and pale. His shoulders slumped, and there was a subtle tremor in his hands that Arthur might have missed if he hadn't been looking so closely.

"How is he?" Colin asked, voice gentle, like anything louder might shatter the silence.

"Sleeping. He seems unharmed."

Colin exhaled as if he'd been holding his breath and raked a hand through his hair, leaving it standing on end. "Good. That's good."

There was a weighty pause as Colin's gaze lingered on the door, and Arthur saw the flicker of something like contrition in the man's face.

"You were right," Colin said, voice tinged with something reluctant, like the words had to be pried loose. "It was a mistake. I shouldn't have sat in that chair. I thought—well, I guess I thought too highly of my own abilities," he huffed with a sardonic smile.

Arthur's jaw tightened. "What abilities exactly?" His tone came out sharper than intended, but the unease gnawing at his ribs made it hard to soften anything.

"I've always been different, you know? Even as a kid, Will says I was weird. Too quiet, too observant. I could always hear things, whispers or intents in people's minds." He shrugged, his shoulder brushing against Arthur's as he took in a deep breath. "The first time I realized I could see ghosts, I was six, and it was at my grandpa's funeral. Isn't that fucked? He was standing by the coffin, and I couldn't understand why everyone was sad if he was right there."

Arthur could picture it — a smaller Colin, thin with enormous eyes and messy hair, glancing around a crowded, somber room in confusion.

"Will was the only one who ever believed me. Actually, I'm not sure he does, but he pretends to, for my benefit. When our parents died, it was awful."

"Could you see them?" he asked despite himself.

Colin shook his head. "No. That was the worst part. I couldn't. They died in a car accident out of town. Will and I weren't with them. I never really got to say goodbye. That's how I started looking into it all," he said. "I'd always ignored it before, the spirits and the voices. But I wanted to see them. So I started researching ways to get in touch."

"Did you?"

"Never," Colin said. "They never answered. But others did. I found a purpose in that. Helping them felt sort of like closure. Grace was my only friend, the only one willing to stick around the weird kid who claimed he could talk to ghosts. Sometimes she helped me, and sometimes she stayed when nobody else would. That was enough."

He hesitated. "Say I believe in, well, any of this," he said, "what do you think is going on here? Really?"

Colin's mouth quirked up at one corner, weary but maybe just a little smug. Colin hedged, "I can't be sure, but I think your father is tethered here."

Arthur arched a brow, giving him the full brunt of his you cannot be serious face. "Oh, come on," he said with a dry laugh.

Colin shrugged, unbothered. "It's not actually unprecedented," he said, tone maddeningly calm. "Spirits rarely get stuck to a place intentionally. They die feeling like they still have work to do, a life to live. So they just…stay."

Arthur let out a long breath, scrubbing a hand down his face. "So my father was such a dick that he couldn't give us the estate even when he was dead, is that it?"

Colin let out a surprised bark of laughter at that. "Well, that's not how I would've put it, but it's likely. Souls attach to locations the same way they do in life. What's a place you love more than anything? The place you would go if you wanted to be the most you?"

Arthur chewed on the thought, ideas flashing through his mind in quick succession: the tiny apartment he used to share with Alex and Theo, the study room he'd claimed in college where he'd spent untold hours pouring over assignments, the high school running track where he had learned to exhaust his anger and frustration in long loops of motion, and finally, the only real answer: the old Ashford stables where he had spent endless hours alone, learning to care for creatures smaller and weaker than himself. It had taught him all the skills August Ashford looked down on: patience, compassion, and the power of vigilance. "The stables," he eventually answered, sure and honest and more open than he'd intended.

Colin smiled and nodded. "I can see that. Caretaking suits you. And of course you're the sort of rich people who have horse stables," he said.

Arthur couldn't stop himself from smiling back at that. "Hah, hah."

"So the stables then. Say you died suddenly, right? You're young, healthy, marginally happy, but you didn't get to live out all your years. You didn't get to fulfill all your dreams: build a career, have a family, that sort of thing. When you die, your soul still longs. It still reaches and wants, even if the body can no longer support it. So it finds the place where it was most fulfilled—the stables for you—"

"And the estate for my father," Arthur said, catching on.

Colin nodded. "Right. And it stays. It's not malicious or conniving; most times, it's stuck and performing as it always did. Unfortunately, your father was a bigoted asshat, so, you know, 'as he always did' is pretty aggressive and shitty."

This time, it was Arthur who barked a surprised laugh,

outright and loud, filling the hall and leaving behind a ringing echo. It was so honest and candid he couldn't help but smile, bending in half with the force of his mirth.

Beside him, Colin smiled softly but then rubbed at his temple and grimaced.

Arthur cleared his throat, trying to bring himself under control, a smile still fighting at the corner of his mouth. "Headache?" he asked Colin, unsurprised after what had happened earlier in the study.

Colin huffed. "It's one of many drawbacks to the whole 'psychic' thing," he said, straightening with squinted eyes like the dim hallway lights had suddenly become too bright. A thin rivulet of blood slipped from his nostril, leaving a bright streak down his lip and chin.

Arthur stiffened. "Colin?"

Colin blinked, swayed, then tried to wave it off with a hand. "It's nothing. Just—" His voice cut off as his knees buckled.

Arthur moved without thinking. One arm caught Colin around the abdomen, the other bracing against his shoulder as the man sagged into him, far too limp, far too cold.

"Colin!" The name tore out louder than Arthur meant, echoing. His panic surged as he shook him once, trying to pull him back. "Colin!"

Colin's head lolled against his shoulder, lashes trembling but eyes shut.

Arthur felt something colder than fear curl in his gut: the realization that his sister might be right.

CHAPTER 14

LANCE

Lance had known Arthur Ashford long before any of this ghost business. The memory was still clear as day: a rain-slick Wednesday night, Lance filling paper cups with terrible coffee in the fluorescent-lit basement of a shelter while Arthur sat across from three queer kids who had nowhere else to go. He hadn't looked like a polished Ashford heir then, just a man in a wrinkled Oxford shirt, tie shoved in his pocket, reading glasses sliding down his nose. Arthur had listened, taken notes in his neat hand, and dismantled the red tape standing between those kids and a place to sleep.

When Lance's nonprofit had gone hunting for a law firm to help them with contracts and liability clauses, Arthur had been his first thought. He'd volunteered on the spot. No fee, no fanfare. He just calmly stepped up, as if it didn't matter that his family name was etched into half the courthouses in the city or that his father had been a staunch supporter of anti-LGBTQ legislation.

Beneath the icy, trust-fund façade Arthur wore like armor, Lance had glimpsed the boy who lived within. A child who had grown up under the thumb of a tyrant but had somehow come out still aching to protect people. The others had only met Arthur's rough edges: the dry quips, the cutting glare, the aristocratic air that could frost a room. But Lance had seen the man in a folding chair, offering legal advice between awkward sips of coffee that tasted of cardboard.

In the two years they'd worked together, Lance had never seen Arthur lose his cool. Not once. Which was why, when he heard Arthur's voice raw and shouting Colin's name, every hair on the back of his neck stood upright.

He and Grace locked eyes for a second, then ran towards the sound. They skidded around the corner to find Arthur on the floor with his arms wrapped around Colin's slack form as if he could anchor him back to consciousness. Blood slicked the psychic's upper lip and chin, stark against his pale skin, and for the first time Lance thought Arthur looked breakable.

"Shit," Lance breathed, dropping beside them. His fingers went instinctively to Colin's wrist, searching. Relief hit like a wave when he found a pulse, faint but steady. It lasted only a heartbeat before the air itself shifted and he was back at fear's doorstep.

The temperature plummeted. The fine hairs on Lance's arms lifted. Grace shivered beside him, her exhale visible in the dim corridor. One by one, the lights along the hallway sputtered and died until only the sconce above Arthur still glowed, casting a sickly yellow cone of light around them. The wallpaper, a dark green damask pattern faded with age, rippled as though something on the other side was straining to get through.

"Do you see that?" Grace asked, her voice thin and brittle with terror.

Lance couldn't answer, but he saw it.

The wall bulged, then split as a gray, long-fingered hand pushed through the plaster. The wall gave way like wet paper as a face pressed forward, half-submerged. Its eyes were pits too deep to hold light. The rest of it followed, staggering free of the wall as though dragged from a grave. It might have been a man, once, but only in how any corpse had once been a person.

Grace's grip latched onto his sleeve, nails biting through the fabric to his skin. "Tell me you see it, Lance."

"I see it." His voice trembled, and the sound of his own fear unsettled him more than the thing itself.

The figure leaned forward, ignoring gravity, ignoring logic. Its lips parted wider, and the whisper hit them like a cold gust: *He is mine now.*

Colin twitched in Arthur's arms, a small, pained flinch, as though the words were digging straight into him.

Something in Lance snapped. He surged to his feet, stepping between the apparition and his friends without thinking. His heart thundered so hard that it hurt. He had no plan, no weapon, nothing but the bone-deep instinct to shield.

Grace moved faster. With shaking hands, she dug into her coat pocket and yanked out a small cloth pouch. Salt. Colin had pressed them on everyone a few days ago, with that calm little smile and the warning they'd all half-dismissed. Lance had laughed. He wasn't laughing now.

Grace's arm snapped out in a shaky arc, scattering the salt across the boards in a jagged line between them and the thing. The grains glimmered in the light like frost.

The figure shrieked soundlessly, its face twisting, body

unraveling into smoke. With a violent shudder, it imploded back into the wall and vanished.

The corridor stilled, and the lights flared weakly back to life.

Arthur exhaled hard, pale and wide-eyed, his voice frayed at the edges. "What the fuck?"

Grace's hands shook so badly she almost dropped the pouch as she shoved it back into her pocket. Her face was bloodless, eyes huge. "We all saw that, right?"

Lance swallowed, still watching the place where the ghost had been. His throat felt scraped raw. "Yeah," he said. "We saw it."

Colin stirred weakly against Arthur's hold, a moan escaping him, and all three of them jumped at the sound.

Grace sagged back against the wall, pressing a trembling hand to her mouth. "It wanted him," she whispered. Her voice cut through the stillness all the same.

The words sent a fresh chill creeping down Lance's spine. He dragged a hand over his face, trying to steady himself, and looked at Arthur. The man's expression was like stone, but he clenched Colin's shirt, turning his knuckles white.

"We need to move him," Lance said. His voice was steady despite his inner turmoil. "Now. Before it comes back."

Arthur snapped his gaze up defensively, as though the suggestion were an accusation. Lance didn't push. He rose slowly, extending a hand. "Come on. Let's get him somewhere safe," he offered, knowing in his bones that the only safety for Colin lay outside Ashford Manor.

Arthur hesitated, then shifted Colin into his arms, rising with surprising grace. He didn't take Lance's hand. He didn't need to. His posture said what his mouth never would: I'm not letting him go.

The three of them moved as a unit, Arthur leading with Colin cradled against him, Grace hovering as though afraid the air itself might split again. Lance brought up the rear, pulse still hammering, eyes darting to every shadow that seemed too deep. The house felt awake and watchful.

"Where?" Arthur asked, not slowing. "Where is safe?"

Lance opened his mouth, then shut it. He wanted to say "outside," scream it if he had to, but he knew that the idea was out of the question. Grace wouldn't leave, not with Theo still in danger, and Colin wouldn't either.

"The sitting room," Grace said, breathless. "He and Will laid down salt lines and sigils when we set up, remember? At least there, it can't cross."

Arthur didn't like it. His expression made that clear, but his options were nonexistent. He adjusted his grip on Colin, the psychic's head lolling against his shoulder, and gave the smallest nod. Lance caught the movement and felt a knot form in his chest. Arthur Ashford, who lived and died by control, was down to following the advice of a twenty-three-year-old grad student with a pouch of salt.

It scared the hell out of him.

And yet when Arthur glanced down at Colin, eyes shadowed, hand cupping the back of his head with unconscious care, Lance thought of that rainy Wednesday night they'd first met in the shelter again. He thought of Arthur, rolling up his sleeves when no one was looking.

Whatever came next, it wasn't just the ghosts Arthur was fighting. It was the house, his father's shadow, and his own fear of losing the first person who'd gotten past his walls.

CHAPTER 15

COLIN

Colin surfaced slowly, like swimming up through syrup, each heartbeat a drumming against his skull. The surrounding air was thick, almost viscous, making his limbs heavy and unresponsive. For a disorienting moment he wasn't sure where he was, or why his feet weren't on the ground, or why the world rocked beneath him, slow and nauseating like the gentle crest of a boat on a storm-dark sea.

Then, Arthur's steady voice cut through the haze closer than Colin expected. "Don't wiggle."

Arthur. Of course. The sound anchored him, and he peeled his eyes open to take in the hallway wavering around him, making his stomach lurch. Dust motes floated like tiny, frantic spirits in the half-light. Grace hovered on his right, her body tense and her fingers twitching as if she wanted to reach out to him.

"Put me down," Colin rasped, his words thin and hoarse.

Arthur's arms only tightened. "Not a chance."

Colin wanted to argue and insist he was fine and could walk himself. But he wasn't, and he couldn't. Something cold and possessive slithered across the back of his neck, making gooseflesh prickle under his skin like needles. His protests died in his throat.

He twisted just enough to glance over Arthur's shoulder and watch the hallway stretch out impossibly long behind them. The shadows lengthened as if they were growing, pulling them further from the promise of safety. With every step Arthur took, the air grew heavier and colder.

"Arthur," Colin said, unsure if he was issuing a warning or a plea.

Arthur didn't slow. "I know."

"It's him," Colin said, throat tight.

"I know," Arthur said, sharper this time, edges like steel. "We saw."

"You saw?" Colin swallowed the instinct to flinch. He had known the moment they'd crossed the threshold of the estate that this one would be different. The drag of something old and ravenous leeched at his strength like tendrils from the structure itself. This house demanded a price, and it had decided it would take it from him. Still, he hadn't told the others. Not Will, not Grace, and certainly not Arthur. August's darkness had entangled Theo too. Colin couldn't leave. Not yet.

The hallway pulsed with menace, floorboards creaking under invisible footsteps, the faint scent of mildew and something metallic curling into his nose. He drew in a shaky breath, tasting the dust and old wood, forcing his eyes to close and trust Arthur to carry him to safety.

When they reached the sitting room, the sounds of life helped to anchor all four of them, and their shoulders dropped in relief. Rain hammered against the tall, leaded windows, sending tiny rivulets running down the glass, and the rolling murmur of thunder vibrated through the floorboards, but warm voices also drifted from the others, mingling with the soft, static hum of electricity that powered all of their electronics. As soon as Arthur guided him through the doorway, the gentle chatter stopped and everyone lurched to their feet.

"Jesus, did you punch him?" Julian shouted.

Will gasped, moving forward with hands outstretched. "Colin, what happened? You're bleeding!"

Arthur's arm tightened around him almost subconsciously. "He fainted," Arthur said, voice steady, a wall against the rising questions. He eased Colin onto the sofa with infuriating gentleness. Colin's vision tugged to the side, shadows folding over themselves so that he could see the threadbare carpet and peeling wallpaper bleeding back into something skeletal, as if the house had peeled back a layer and he could see its very bones.

Arthur's hand tightened on his shoulder. "Don't."

Colin blinked up at him. "Don't what?"

"Don't look at it," Arthur said, jaw locked tight. "It wants you."

A different shiver skittered down Colin's spine. He dragged his gaze away from the corners of the room, where shadows pooled like wet ink, and noticed the others' tension like a live current in the air. He rubbed his face, grimacing as blood from his chin smeared under his fingertips. "Okay," he said, voice hoarse. "I think one of you needs to tell me what happened."

No one moved for a moment. Grace's knuckles were white around the remnants of her bag of salt, Lance had stopped pacing, staring at the shadows pooling beneath the furniture like they might twitch, and Julian and Will edged closer, eager for information.

Arthur broke first. "It came out of the wall," he said, clipped, clinical, as if delivering a testimony in a courtroom. "*He* came out of the wall."

Colin's stomach lurched. "August?"

"In-so-much as that thing could be called my father," Arthur said, nodding grimly.

"He manifested?"

Grace let out a short, brittle laugh, pushing hair from her face, trembling. "*Manifested*? It crawled out of the wall like a fucking nightmare. Don't tell me this is normal, Colin. That was not normal!"

"It's never normal," Colin said, more to himself than to her, head pounding, as if the thing had left fingerprints on his skull. "Did he do anything?"

"Yeah," Lance said, voice rough. His eyes flicked to Colin, assessing. "He told us you were his. Like you were some kind of—" He broke off, raking a hand through his hair.

"Target," Arthur supplied flatly.

Colin swallowed hard, throat thick. That lined up with the cold that had pressed against his spine and the voice he could still hear in his head whispering 'mine' in a voice that wasn't his.

"Fuck," he said, the weight pressing down like the storm outside, relentless and insistent.

For a long moment, all that filled the room was the patter of rain, the distant rumble of thunder, and the static tension between them. Then, loud and unignorable, his stomach gave a gurgling growl that was almost obscene in the thick, haunted air.

Colin grimaced, cheeks coloring. "Um… how about dinner?" he

asked sheepishly, stomach growling again with perfect comedic timing.

The tension cracked, shattering like a dropped vase. Laughter erupted from all corners: Julian, loud and unrestrained; Grace with a shaky snort-laugh, and even Arthur's lips twitched in the faintest hint of exasperated amusement. Colin sank back into the sofa cushions, allowing a small, genuine smile to slip past his fear. Here at least, people would fight for him.

"I'll order something in," Arthur said, pulling out his phone with a roll of his eyes that spoke volumes.

"Chinese," Colin said hopefully.

Relief and cheers erupted in equal measure from the others.

"Chinese, it is," Arthur replied, with almost fond annoyance. Colin smiled in victory, small though it was. "Don't forget to order dumplings," he insisted. "M'just gonna close my eyes for a bit."

The house still hummed beneath his skin, a constant tug of unease, but when Arthur's hand brushed his shoulder again, firm and grounding, Colin let himself sleep. It was the closest thing to peace Colin had felt in days.

CHAPTER 16

WILL

The rain hammered against the tall, leaded windows in steady sheets, the rumble of distant thunder vibrating through the floorboards and walls. Every rumble made the house groan in its old bones. The storm set Will's teeth on edge, but the sitting room felt insulated against the outside world. The scent of soy sauce and ginger curled lazily through the air, mingling with the faint smoke of the fire in the hearth. Cardboard takeout containers lay strewn across the coffee table, punctuated by haphazard piles of napkins and chopsticks, forming a chaotic little nest of domestic normalcy that was almost laughable in a place like this.

Theo, wan and sluggish, but obedient enough, had come down from his bedroom at Alexandra's anxious insistence. He slumped into the armchair nearest the fire, a blanket wrapped around him, and picked at a carton of lo mein with the distracted, half-hearted care of someone who wasn't really awake. Will noted the slight tremor in his hands, the way the firelight caught on his pale cheeks, and tried to let himself relax into the bubble of comfort and care they had created here, though he knew it was a fragile shield against the darkness they faced.

He kept himself at Colin's side, every instinct screaming to stay within reach. His brother looked terrible. Pale, thinner than usual, with dark circles etched under his eyes as if the house had been clawing at him for months rather than days. Will was familiar with psychic interference and how it could affect the younger man, but he'd never seen it so severe or so sudden. The dried blood along his chin caught the firelight and made him look macabre, almost unreal. Will felt a hollow ache coil in his stomach, the helpless urge to scoop Colin up, wrap him in blankets, and carry him far from this cursed place. Anywhere safe. Anywhere else.

But Colin wouldn't allow it, and Will knew the manor had already claimed him in its grip. There was no escaping without a fight, and Colin wouldn't walk away, not from this, not from Theo.

So Will did the only thing he could: he became the mother bird.

"Hey," he said, nudging a cardboard container closer. "Carbs. Protein. Calories. Actual sustenance."

Colin lifted his head lazily, lips parting with a weak protest. "I am literally eating," he whined, lifting a single noodle on his chopsticks as proof.

Will's jaw tightened. He crossed his arms, trying to ignore the faint tremor in his hands. "I swear to God, Col, I will feed you like an infant if I have to." He plopped a dumpling into the container Colin was picking at.

"I'm fairly certain I was breastfed as an infant," Colin said petulantly.

Grace snorted, laughter bubbling out despite the tension. Will ignored her. "You wouldn't know. You were basically a potato when you were born. Head all knobby, like it was growing ears."

Arthur and Julian both erupted in laughter at that, and while Colin tried to muster a glare, it was more tired than intimidating.

Colin lifted a lazy hand and didn't stop Will from pushing another container into it. "I'm just not that hungry," he said.

"You are," Will said, his voice softening despite his frustration, "down past the nausea this place is creating. You just fought something impossible, Colin, and it's not over. You need strength. You need..." He trailed off, glancing at the gaunt lines of Colin's face. "...you need to eat before you collapse. I won't let you kill yourself."

Colin conceded, picking up a dumpling like it was medicine he had to swallow.

Julian, perched on the settee across from them, snorted through a spring roll. "I've never seen anyone bullied into eating dumplings before."

Arthur gave a huff of his own annoyance. "I've never seen anyone so stubbornly unwilling to care for themselves."

Colin rolled his eyes but took another pointed bite. For a fleeting moment, Will allowed himself to forget the darkness pressing in, the way it seeped into corners and dripped beneath doors.

And then the lights flickered.

Meters screamed, monitors beeped, and static crackled through the speakers of their recording equipment until the very air vibrated against Will's skin. His stomach tightened. He scanned the room, eyes darting over the familiar furniture and the firelight dancing across the surface.

"He's crossed the sigils!" Colin said, flinging his food aside in a tangle of noodles and vegetables. He clamped his hands over his ears as if the sound were a physical force ripping through him.

Theo moved. One moment slumped in the chair, and then he stood upright, rigid and still. The roaring fire behind him framed his silhouette, and he took strange, stilted steps toward his mother as she went to her knees before him.

"Theo? Sweetheart?"

Theo shook his head, movements too stiff and precise to be natural. A chill crawled up his spine as the boy's eyes swept over his mother without seeing, lips twisting into a cruel, alien smile, eyes a deep, inky black.

"Filth," Theo spat, voice unfamiliar. "Vermin defile my halls. Traitors. He turned to his mother, who stood frozen in place. "You," he said, "whore! Sullying our bloodline with every breath you take. You were nothing but a pawn, a pretty body to be bartered, and you failed even at that. A viper in my garden."

Alexandra flinched as if struck, but her chin lifted, jaw tight.

Arthur was already moving, stepping between her and Theo's rage. "That's enough."

Theo's lips twisted into a cruel smile. The voice deepened further, echoing so loudly the windows rattled. "And you," he sneered, "my *son*. My heir. Weak. Bent. A disgrace. Fawning after men while you let this house rot. You'll never be fit to carry my name. You'd rather bend your back for another man than bear the Ashford line."

Will could almost see the words hit against Arthur like a physical force. The chill in the room wasn't just rage; it was *August*, clawing at the world beyond the grave, terrified that his children would not preserve the Ashford legacy he had built with an iron hand. Every insult, every accusation, every demand for obedience echoed with the authority of a father who believed survival meant control, that any deviation from his rigid vision would doom them all.

Silence roared in the room, broken only by the fire guttering in the hearth, spitting sparks across the rug. Theo reached out to grab Arthur, but Colin was already on his feet and pushing between them. Will's hands shot out as the air went frigid, and something cold and malicious crawled like ice across his skin.

"Stop," Colin said, voice commanding though his knees shook and hands trembled.

"You've brought scum into my home," Theo continued, turning his knife-sharp gaze around the room to take in Julian, Lance, Grace, and Will. "Dogs dressed as men. Mutts. Foreign trash. Parasites gnawing at the bones of the Ashford legacy."

Colin ignored the words, reaching into his pocket and pulling free his piece of white chalk. Keeping himself stationed just in front of Theo, he began drawing symbols onto his own palms. He threw the chalk aside and pressed one hand onto Theo's forehead.

Theo bucked, strength inhuman, voice jagged and echoing. "You dare—"

"I dare," Colin said with finality. His other hand flared against Theo's chest, golden light spiraling from his palms.

For a heartbeat, the room glowed. The firelight bent toward them, the curtains fluttered, and the air stank of ozone and iron. Theo's mouth opened in a scream that wasn't his own—black smoke writhing up his throat in ragged tendrils. It tore through the house, cracking plaster in jagged lines across the ceiling. The floor shuddered beneath their feet.

Theo collapsed, small and sobbing, into Alexandra's arms. But relief was fleeting and fragile. The house moaned, every board groaning like vertebrae stretching. Windows rattled; the static from their equipment surged to a scream again.

Colin staggered, skin too hot, lips pale, knees giving out. Will lunged, but Arthur caught him, hauling him upright. Colin sagged between them, breath shallow, a trickle of blood slipping from his nose again.

"Christ, he's burning up," Will choked, pressing his palm to Colin's fever-bright cheek.

Theo whimpered into his mother's shoulder, lips moving again, whispering words too to hear. Will leaned closer, the hair on his arms rising.

"...not gone," Theo breathed, but the voice came from all around them, deep and resonant, the manor itself throwing August's obsession through the boy. The fury, the cruelty, the terror—it was the voice of a father who had loved his family only by forcing them into his vision of perfection, terrified that anything less would let the Ashford line crumble.

The fire guttered out with a hiss. Darkness swallowed the room, dense and absolute.

And Will knew, with cold certainty, that Colin had banished nothing.

CHAPTER 17

ALEX

The house had gone unnervingly still after the chaos. Cold, too, as if whatever darkness had clawed through Theo had left a chill stitched into the very air. Alex moved through the rooms like a restless shadow, checking locks that were already latched, testing doors that wouldn't budge. Her hands needed something to do, or she might start unraveling. She had tried to sleep, curled against Theo in his bed like she hadn't since he was a toddler, but her mind refused rest. So she stalked through the halls.

Her circuit of the ground floor brought her to the kitchen, where a faint pool of yellow light spilled across the counters. Grace had her brow furrowed in concentration as she hunched over her laptop and spread of papers in careful chaos. She wore her thick, dark hair in a messy braid over one shoulder, and perched a pair of reading glasses on her head.

"I thought everyone had gone to bed," Alex whispered.

Grace looked up, startled and a little guilty, as if caught sneaking cookies rather than immersing herself in research. "I tried. Couldn't. After all that—" she gestured vaguely toward the sitting room where they'd witnessed the impossible just a few hours earlier. "I figured I'd put the time to use," Grace sighed tiredly.

Alex studied her. Grace's voice was steady, but her shoulders were tight, eyes shadowed with worry.

"Is it always this intense?" Alex asked after a pause. "The investigations, I mean?"

Grace bit her lip, chewing on the thought before sighing. "Colin has always been different, ever since we were kids. I've seen him overwrought before, but like this? Only once and never so suddenly."

"When?"

Grace grimaced. "We had a neighbor haunting him for a few months. We were fourteen."

"Fourteen!"

Grace nodded, offering no further explanation.

Alexandra let the thought turn over in her mind, imagining a younger, more fragile Colin weighed down by forces nobody else could see or fight. Wordlessly, she crossed the room and pulled out a chair. The scrape of wood against tile sounded loud in the house's hush as she sat down beside Grace.

"I..." she began, her voice quieter than intended, catching Grace's attention. Grace looked up, brows knitting in concern. "I was terrified to come back here," she said.

Grace's hands stilled over her computer keys. "It's a lot," she said in understanding.

Alex swallowed, letting the words come in fragments. "We

didn't really have a choice. I've been a single mother since I was eighteen. Things got better when Arthur…but even then, we can't always live on his money. He's worked so hard to rebuild himself into the man he is after our father…anyway, I thought maybe this place could be a new start for all of us, you know? I thought the three of us could make it a home in a way it had never been before."

The admission left a hollow ache in her heart. Shame and fear mingled in her throat, a knot she hadn't allowed herself to name before.

"But being here, all I feel is… small," Alex said. "August Ashford, even dead, is still here, and I can't protect my son from him. I can't protect myself from him. I never could."

Grace reached out and laid a hand over hers. It was gentle, grounding, but it sent warmth creeping into Alex. "You've done more than anyone could have expected," Grace said. "You've survived him, survived this house, and you're still standing. That counts for something."

Alex's throat tightened, and she gave a humorless laugh. "I don't feel like it counts for anything." She hesitated, then shook her head. "I didn't tell Arthur, but a few years ago, after Arthur moved in with me, August found us. He wrote to me asking for a picture of Theo. It was stupid to send one back, but I thought maybe he wanted to repent or get to know his grandson. Then he sent more letters." She shivered at the memory. "They were vile. He said I had 'tainted the Ashford line' and called Theo an *abomination*. He said I was the reason Arthur had 'gone wrong.' It was so cruel and unnecessary. We'd washed our hands of him, and he'd washed his hands of us. Why did he reach out just to be hateful?"

"A picture?"

Alex nodded. "They were obsessive, honestly, towards the end. I guess maybe it was his mind slipping, but at the time I didn't know he was ill and I just thought he was going insane. He kept saying all this nonsense about bloodline ties and legacies. He wanted to punish me for leaving the family. And now it feels like the darkness he left behind will do just that."

Grace pulled one of the surrounding books closer. She flipped it open and began rifling through the pages, eyes widening as she found whatever it was she was looking for. "Alex, was this the picture you sent him?" she asked, voice bright with something like epiphany. She turned the book to face Alex, and it was only then that she realized it was some sort of journal. Her father's messy scrawl was unmistakable as it skated across the page in fine, looped letters. Pasted in the middle of the page was a photo of Theo around seven years old, a front tooth missing and his eyes bright.

"Oh," she said. "He kept it?"

"He did," Grace nodded, chewing her lip. "And I think I know what he was going to do with it." Grace flipped through the pages quickly, her finger tracing the looping scrawl of August's handwriting. "Look at this," she said, tilting the journal toward Alex. "There are notes here about a ritual. See these symbols?" She pointed to faint circular sketches interspersed between paragraphs of wild rambling. "He wanted to amplify his influence and tie himself to the house and his descendants. Theo, you, Arthur. It's not a residual haunting at all; he planned this. That's why he left you in the will."

Alex felt the room tilt, the warmth seeping out like air from a punctured balloon. Her stomach lurched at the thought: all along, she'd assumed August's malice had been spiritual and psychological: a lingering ghost of his ego. But now it seemed purposeful and well-orchestrated.

"He's using us to stay in the house," Alex said, voice barely audible.

Grace nodded, biting her lip. "I think so. And the ritual amplifies whatever psychic resonance Colin has. That's why he collapsed earlier. That's why Theo's vulnerable to it. It's like August built a trap designed to exploit them."

Alex shivered, pulling her cardigan tighter around her body. The vulnerability she had been holding at bay, the fear of losing Theo, suddenly overwhelmed her.

"I need to tell Colin," Grace said, snapping the journal shut and rising to her feet. "Now. We need to deal with this quickly, before the strain takes anymore out of him."

Alex followed her, heart thundering, throat tight. "But he's already so weak."

"All the more reason," Grace insisted. "If we wait, he'll push himself too far again. He's already giving everything to protect Theo and us. We can't let him carry this alone. Not when August's obsession is literally reaching through the house into him."

CHAPTER 18

GRACE

Grace shifted from foot to foot, vibrating with energy despite the late hour and the exhaustion clawing at her ankles and shoulders like chains. The study was dim, lit only by a single lamp perched on a cluttered desk, throwing long, angular shadows across the room lined with tall, leather-bound books. The weak light of the slowly rising dawn poured in through the cracked window. Outside, the rain had slowed to a persistent drizzle, leaving the garden drenched and the stone paths slick.

The others looked like they had been dragged from their beds, their eyes heavy, their shoulders drooping. Arthur leaned against the far wall, arms crossed, jaw tight, eyes vigilant and flicking with rapid, controlled glances around the room. Alexandra sat on the edge of the desk, alert and watchful, the faint gleam of the lamp catching the sculpted planes of her face. Julian had given up all pretense, still half-dozing upright on the floor. Will stood stiffly at the door, the only other person alert, his jaw working, annoyance radiating from him like heat.

Grace ignored the subtle grumbles and the wary, tired stares. "This isn't just a residual spirit," she said, gratified that the group all came more to attention at the words. "I've been going through August's journals and letters, and I think I've figured out why he's lingering here."

Arthur raised an eyebrow, voice cautious. "And why is that?"

"August wasn't just obsessively ideological about bloodlines," Grace said, pacing a few steps across the rug, her voice rising with fervor. "He was performing rituals to physically tie himself to this house. He wanted to anchor his presence here, to bind himself to the foundations of his ancestral home. This is a *possession*."

"Of a building?" Julian asked, skeptical, tilting his head so that the shadow flickered across his bemused features. "That's new, even for us."

"Also nearly impossible," Will said, arms crossed, his face pinched with disbelief. "The amount of psychic energy it would take to hold that level of control over—" He cut off, eyes snapping toward Colin with a flash of horror.

Colin sighed, the sound heavy with weary acceptance, and nodded. "That would explain some things," he said.

Arthur's eyes widened, fingers tightening into fists at his sides. His disbelief was plain, but so was the horror settling behind it, darkening his usual composure. The others arrived at the conclusion a half-step behind. Julian let out a nervous whistle, and Lance rubbed his face with both hands.

"So every second Colin spends in this house is dangerous?" Will asked soberly.

"And Theo," Colin added regretfully, his eyes shadowed. "Every hour we delay, the bindings grow stronger, and the house itself becomes more hostile."

Grace nodded, feeling a swell of urgency tighten her chest. "Exactly. This isn't theoretical. The house *is* a trap. A carefully constructed one."

The room fell into tense silence for a moment, punctuated only by the soft drip of water from the eaves outside.

"So we should leave," Will said, practical and sure, though the edge in his voice betrayed the weariness he'd been masking.

"We can't," Colin grimaced, eyes flicking toward the floor as he rubbed the bridge of his nose. "I'm too tied in. So is Theo. We could escape the property, but we're more likely to drag him with us than break the hold."

"Fuck," Julian raged.

Colin nodded. "We have to break the connection to leave."

"How can we do that?" Alexandra asked, voice tight with tension.

"I think there's an entrance to a ritual room somewhere in this study," Grace said. "We need to find it. It's the source of his ties to the property and the only place we can break them."

The group spread out across the study to search. Alexandra ran her fingers along the bookshelves, tapping spines for hidden switches. Lance gingerly probed the room, frowning as he tested each panel and molding.

Grace circled the desk, August's journal clutched tight in her hand. She had spent hours with the man's rambling prose, but one page had lodged itself in her mind like a burr. She flipped it open now, fingers tracing the line of ink scrawled in a fevered hand: *Where the serpent hides its head, the lion guards the flame. Beneath the father's watchful eye, blood will open the way.*

Her pulse quickened. She scanned the room until her gaze

snagged on the family crest carved into the heavy mahogany desk, a fire-breathing lion rampant with a serpent for a tail. Her breath caught.

"It's here," she whispered. "The journal says that the entrance has something to do with the desk. Something about the serpent's head and the lion's flame."

Julian perked up from his chair, pulling his thermal camera from his bag with a smirk. "Well, let's see what's warm and toasty." He swept the lens across the walls, the shelves, and the floor. Most of the study bled out in shades of dull blue and gray. But when he passed the camera across the desk, a single point on the paneling behind it flared bright orange. "Gotcha," he said, tapping the screen. "Hotspot, dead center. Something's burning energy behind that wall."

The others closed in, tension tightening the air like a noose. Arthur stepped forward, his expression carved in stone. He crouched at the desk, fingers brushing the underside. "My father loved theatrics," he said, voice bitter. "Always had to build his secrets into puzzles. The mechanism won't be obvious." He traced the carved lion crest with his fingertips, jaw tight. Then, with a grimace of recognition, he pressed one thumb hard against the lion's eye.

A click echoed.

With a groan, the panel behind the desk shifted. The wooden slats slid apart in a grinding protest, and a draft of stale air rushed into the study. Iron and old wax filled the air. The lamplight flickered as though reluctant to enter.

Darkness cloaked the room beyond. Faint shafts of dawn light from the study just reached the depths, illuminating the strange, angular symbols etched directly into the stone. Faint traces of chalk lingered, ghostly white against the gray, and Grace's pulse quickened as she took in the lines of a spell meant to bind and anchor. A thrill of dread and exhilaration rose in her. This was it. The heart of August's work. The source of the binding.

Arthur stepped forward, his movements careful, almost hesitant, disbelief and horror etched clearly into his rigid posture. "Christ," he breathed, as if louder words might awaken the malevolent presence within the stone. "He built it right under our noses."

Grace swallowed, lips dry, and nodded toward the threshold where the room pulled against her skin like invisible fingers. Alexandra joined them, her eyes flicking from symbol to symbol, each etching a silent warning. "How do we undo it?" she asked uncertainly.

"I should go in," Colin said, stepping forward, drawing everyone back from the secret room, his gaze steady though the exhaustion in his frame betrayed him.

"Like hell," Will said, stepping between Colin and the passage. Arthur mirrored his stance with a firm glare.

Colin lifted his lips in a half-hearted, tired smile at their instinctive protectiveness, but even that gesture was faint, and his eyes fluttered shut. "I'm sorry to pull the 'I'm special card' here," he said, voice rasping. "But does anyone else have latent psychic powers that can close a gate?"

Julian moved closer, placing a tentative hand on Colin's shoulder. "I'd be willing to try," he said, his usual swagger dampened by concern. "Jokes aside, Col, you look terrible. I think you're already on death's door."

"He's right," Will said, stepping in closer, arms folded tight. "You can't possibly do this right now. You don't even look like you can make it across the room."

"Maybe we wait until morning," Alexandra said hesitantly, glancing at the faint light of dawn already creeping through the tall windows. "Or evening? A few hours of sleep might—"

"He won't regain strength with rest," Grace said firmly, apologetic but unwavering. "Nothing will restore him at this point. Not sleep, not food, not time. The design of this house prevents it."

Colin's gaze dropped to the floor for a moment before lifting to meet hers, haunted. "You're right," he said. "I thought if I could distract him, I could pull his attention off Theo. I thought it might weaken the hold, and then I could get him to let go of me too. It's a clever design. Every ounce of energy I've poured into this place, with will or word, has made the trap stronger. It was created for someone like me."

The group shifted uneasily, the room thick with the weight of realization. It brought with it a suffocating mixture of fear and urgency that made her fingers tremble against her notebook. The house felt alive, breathing around them as if it was calculating its last move.

Then, a voice cut through the tension like a shard of ice.

"Or someone like me."

They all twisted, and Grace realized Theo must have woken and found them here. The boy moved in silence and now stood behind them, his eyes curiously fixed on the room beyond.

"No, Theo," Colin said, his voice trembling.

"You can't do it," the boy insisted, taking a step back. "That leaves me."

"You're too young," Colin countered.

Theo scowled impatiently. "How old were you?" he asked as

if frustrated at being coddled. There was no malice in it, just blunt observation, a wisdom Grace didn't expect from someone so young. She caught herself wondering if Theo's connection gave him true insight into Colin's past, or if he was simply sharper than anyone gave him credit for.

"Theo, we don't know what will happen if you go into that room," Grace said, stepping into his line of sight, her own chest tightening as her heart pounded against her ribs.

"Please, sweetheart," Alexandra said, voice trembling with urgency and maternal worry. She took a tentative step forward, hand outstretched. "Please, Theo, let's just talk. We'll figure something else out so that you—"

Theo's expression hardened, the soft curiosity replaced by a depth beyond his years. His eyes now gleamed with dark understanding.

"I'm sorry, Mom," he said, a strange calm settling over him. He gave a single, steadying nod, resolute and final, before stepping back through the open doorway and into the ritual room.

The door slid shut behind him with a soft, grinding thud, leaving the group staring into the empty frame, the silence stretching thick and suffocating.

And then the screaming started.

CHAPTER 19

COLIN

Colin's stomach churned, a tightening knot of dread that had nothing to do with his fatigue. The sounds of panic were a raw, clawing echo in his ears: Will's frustrated shouts, Julian and Lance's grunts, the thud of bodies against the heavy wooden panel. Arthur's voice, strained and panicked, rose above the others, calling out Theo's name. And louder still were Theo's own terrified screams, fractured and desperate, bouncing back at them from the shadows behind the false wall.

Colin's heart slammed against his ribs. Grace crouched beside Alexandra, her hand firm against the other woman's shoulder, murmuring soothing words that were almost drowned out by the noise. Alexandra's chest heaved, sobs wracking her frame, her hands clutching the desk like it might somehow anchor her. Colin's throat tightened at the sight, the rawness of her fear and helplessness stabbing deeper than any other emotion in the room.

Colin's voice cut through the chaos like a blade, unnervingly calm in contrast to the frantic energy around him. "That won't work." The other men froze mid-push, bodies pressed against the door, trying to wrest it open with sheer force of will. "It'll have to be me."

The room held its breath. Julian and Lance stepped back reluctantly, chests heaving and eyes darting between Colin and the door. Arthur and Will, however, still blocked the path.

"You aren't strong enough for this," Will said forcefully. "It will *kill* you, Colin!"

"Better me than the boy," Colin said.

Arthur's gaze met his, worry deeply etched in the lines on his face. "I'm coming in with you," he said.

Colin shook his head. "It's too dangerous."

"For both of us," Arthur said. "I'm not asking, Colin. It's my house and my asshole father. If you're going to sacrifice yourself, I'm going to pull you back."

The words were gruff and hard, but the softness of the gesture broke something free in Colin. In another world, he would've kissed Arthur, just once, just to know what he'd be missing, but Theo's screams were only pitching higher and time was running out.

Instead, he nodded his acceptance and reached out, lacing his fingers into Arthur's warm, callused palms. Will stepped back with a choked-off sob, and Colin took his place.

He drew in a few slow, deliberate breaths, letting the steady rhythm center him. He could feel the pulse of the room, the lingering residue of August's rituals threading through the foundation, the air vibrating with tension. And beyond that, deeper still, was the raw, fractured psychic energy of Theo screaming in fear and confusion.

He stepped forward and raised his hand to the door. Nothing about the thick wood differed from before, nothing that should allow it to yield. And yet, with effortless motion, he pushed.

The door swung open as though it had been waiting for him all along, clattering off its track and falling into the shadowed room beyond with a deafening thud.

Colin stepped into the room, and the shadows pressed back. His breathing quickened as something dense and stifling gathered around him, tugging his mind like hands made of smoke.

Theo was in the center of the chamber, his slight form curled into a tight ball and crying out in high, desperate wails. The surrounding floor glowed with concentric circles of chalked sigils, holding him in place.

"August," Colin called, voice steady despite the churn of dread twisting in his stomach. "I know what you've been doing here. I know how you've tied yourself to this house."

The response came not as sound, but as a vibration in the air, the whisper of a voice folding around his consciousness: cold, commanding, impossibly large. "Ah, the meddling psychic," it said, laughter rippling through the walls. "So curious, so persistent."

Arthur's hand gripped tighter around his. "You've been siphoning him," Colin said, each word measured. "Using him to fuel this trap you made for him. But how did you know he had the gift?"

Abruptly the screaming ceased, leaving a thundering silence in its wake. Theo went still where he'd been curled on the floor and pushed himself up to standing in strange, stilted motions. "I cursed him with the gift myself," Theo said in a voice that wasn't his own. "I knew my children would not carry on our line nobly," he cast a dismissive look at Arthur and scoffed. "A queer and a whore. Shame on the Ashford name. I began looking into ways to keep the line pure by refusing to pass it to either of them, but first I needed a vessel to channel into."

"So you pressed yourself onto an ancestral foundation," Colin nodded his understanding.

Theo smirked, too wide and wicked to be fully human. "Yes, but I needed a source of energy. So I created one." He waved his hand down the slight frame and laughed, high and wicked. "This mutt of a human wouldn't have been my first choice, but it had to be of direct bloodline. So I placed a curse using his photo, and I drew him to the house to help sustain my tie to the estate."

"But a house, even a grand estate with a spirit inside of it, is not the same as living." Colin argued.

"Quite," he conceded, stalking towards Colin like a tiger with prey in its sight. "But with enough time, enough influence—"

Colin trembled. "You're hollowing him out," he realized, horrified, "You're emptying him so that you can inhabit his body."

The room tilted around Colin, tightening and pressing against him. He felt every heartbeat of Theo within the house, each one a thread in August's insidious design. Now, he understood how cruel it was: August never meant Theo to leave this place or grow beyond it. August kept close watch over every moment of Theo's life and every ounce of his untapped potential, laying a careful foundation for a power grab years in the making.

"I had planned for all of it," August said as though he was reaching into Colin's mind and reading it. "But you? You were such a delicious surprise. Your power has hastened the process by years. Now? This vessel is almost ready."

Colin's stomach dropped. The boy's terror and confusion

echoed around the room. Colin would not allow him to be consumed.

"Take me instead," he said, ignoring Arthur's cry of surprise beside him. "Take me. You can do more, accomplish more in an adult body than a child ever could. You need energy, right? Use me and leave the boy be."

The silence stretched. Then, with a rumbling chuckle, Theo stepped into Colin's face. "You presume too much, meddling psychic. You have no blood ties. No claim. Your vessel will not open for me as his does. Tempting though the offer is."

A surge of dark power pushed against him, as if August was testing him, tasting him. Colin's chest tightened, but he drew a deliberate, slow breath and let it curl around him. "I am more than a vessel," he said. "Blood isn't the only thing that matters. Power matters. Skill. Knowledge. Control."

A surge of laughter rolled through the stone, dark and mocking. "Foolish boy. You think arrogance can replace lineage? You cannot—"

"I don't think," Colin interrupted, voice rising over the mocking tones. "I know. I feel it. I know how this house breathes, how it clings to the boy. I know where you've planted your threads, and I can pull them free." He stepped closer, letting his presence fill the chamber. "Every ounce of energy you've siphoned, every moment you've bound him, I can take it into my own."

The surrounding air thickened, the walls groaning as if aware of the defiance. Shadows rippled like dark water. "If you pry him free, it will only entrap you in his stead. You really wish to take his place?" August asked with a mixture of incredulity and cautious intrigue.

Colin's fingers clenched, drawing on every thread of his own power, every memory of the discipline that had kept him alive and sane. "If I pull him free," he said, "you let him leave. That is the deal, August Ashford. My abilities for his life."

August, still wearing the child's body like an ill-fitting suit, tilted his head in consideration. "Deal," he said after a long beat, "but the entrapment will take you as soon as he is free. There's no backing out."

Colin knew that too. The sigils called, even now, to capture his life force and ensnare it. His spirit in the center of this mechanism would be like using a solar flare to run a flashlight, and he trembled at the thought of what August could do with that much power. Still, the house contained the boy's soul — fractured, raw, and very frightened.

Arthur's hand squeezed his, grounding him in reality, even as the room bent to the will of ancient, twisted darkness. Colin turned to him, steady gaze cutting through the haze of panic and dread that clung to the edges of the room. "When I break the connection," he said resolutely, "get Theo out of here. Whatever happens next, he has to be safe."

Arthur's jaw tightened, fingers flexing with unspoken protest, but Colin gave him a single, firm nod, a signal of his absolute trust. Colin released Arthur's hand without another word and positioned his feet in the space marked by a single chalked sigil: *entrapment.*

The warmth and the grounding reassurance vanished from his consciousness, leaving him alone with the raw, malignant spirit coiled in the room. He reached out with his mind, finding the tattered threads of Theo's presence running through the stones, and he welcomed it, letting it spiral around him in gentle touches.

It hit him instantly; a pressure like a tidal wave began clawing up his limbs, and a suffocating weight pressed against every nerve and sinew. Colin drew a slow, steadying breath and opened his arms, almost as if to embrace the darkness itself. The psychic tendrils snaked around him, probing, testing, lashing out. But Colin met them willingly. He let the malevolent energy wash over him, let it pour into his mind, and began prying Theo free of the tethers.

It was like trying to wrest a living thing from the bones of the earth, and the house groaned in response, shivering, the symbols carved into the stone flaring as if they were alive.

Colin's entire being burned with the intensity of August's energy, a dark fire that threatened to consume him if he faltered. He held the current, shaping it, bending it, turning it into a conduit and accepting it into his own body.

He knew the exact moment Theo broke free by the sudden impact of taking the entire entity into his being, as their shared burden became just his. His knees buckled, and he hit the stone hard, sparks of pain jolting through his body and mingling with the inferno tearing through his veins. Every breath seared his lungs; every heartbeat thundered like it might break him apart.

Colin grit his teeth, vision swimming, but forced himself to stay steady. His arms trembled as the tendrils coiled tighter, twisting into him like roots digging into soil. He wanted to scream, to claw the invading presence out of his skull, but he didn't. He anchored himself in the feel of Arthur's hand in his, the radiance of Grace's smile, Will's steady presence, and Julian's boisterous laughter.

"This isn't your house anymore," he rasped, though blood beaded from his mouth and eyes, tracing fiery trails down his face. "It isn't your body. And it sure as hell won't be your future."

The shadows shrieked in response; the walls trembled so violently that dust rained from above. The sigil beneath Colin flared brilliant white beneath the layers of chalk and ash. Behind him, he could sense Arthur seize Theo by the shoulders, hauling him backwards and out of the ritual room. He sagged momentarily in relief.

"You want my power?" Colin gasped, his voice carrying over the roar of collapsing stone. His eyes burned, light spilling from them in thin, jagged cracks. "You can fucking choke on it."

He flung open every door inside himself, every chamber of his mind, every scar, every wound he had ever endured, and pulled. He dragged August deeper, locking the malignant presence behind the fortification of his own psyche, sealing each chain with fire and will. As the tether broke, the house groaned, beams shattered, and the sigils erupted. Colin's throat tore from the strain of his last scream when he imprisoned August within his mind.

Then he let death take him.

CHAPTER 20

ARTHUR

The boy was safe. Arthur clung to the thought as he half-carried, half-dragged Theo into Alexandra's waiting arms. She folded the child against her as though he were still an infant; her face stricken with relief. Grace and Lance closed in protectively, murmuring reassurances.

Arthur turned back toward the ritual room. Colin hadn't come out.

The realization hit like a fist in his ribs, stealing his breath. If Colin wasn't coming out on his own, then…Arthur's throat closed on the thought. He couldn't let it finish.

Behind him, the other's voices rose in a panicked chorus, hands grabbing at him, trying to pull him out of the room. He barely registered who was shouting what, only the raw edge of fear in their voices.

He shoved them toward the study door, movements harsh, almost violent. "Go. Get out!" Arthur said, the command more roar than words.

They balked, as if sheer refusal could anchor him there with them, but then the ceiling above gave a long, aching groan. Dust sifted down in a slow curtain, catching in their hair, their lashes, turning them pale as ghosts. The timbers creaked again, loud and awful, like the bellow of some dying beast giving way.

The sound went straight through Arthur's chest, hollowing him out. This house wasn't just wounded. It was breaking. If he didn't move now, the house would bury Colin.

The ritual chamber reeked of burnt hair and scorched stone as he returned to it. Fire blackened the walls, and the chalk circle lay in ruins, symbols smeared to ash. In the middle of it was Colin, limbs limp, body twisted like a discarded marionette.

For a terrible heartbeat, Arthur froze. The collapsing house roared around him, but all he could hear was his own rush of blood.

A crack overhead snapped him back, and he lunged into action, scooping Colin's slack body over his shoulder with a grunt that was half-effort, half-curse.

"You idiot," he rasped, not sure if he meant Colin or himself.

Arthur staggered out of the study with Colin's weight dragging him down. The world shrank to grit, smoke, and the pounding of his own pulse. The walls groaned and beams split with each step, as if the house knew it was about to die, and he was trespassing on its final breaths. The ground trembled beneath them, a deep groan rolling outward from the manor's foundations.

And then Ashford Manor died.

The great bones of the house went first: the grand staircase split down its center, a jagged wound that sent carved balusters tumbling like teeth knocked from a jaw. The crystal chandelier in the front room snapped from its chain and fell, shattering across the marble floor with a great crash.

The windows burst outward in a storm of glass, each pane shrieking like a voice freed. Walls bowed, groaned, and then collapsed inward, like ribs caving around a failing heart. The roof sagged, then folded with a long, mournful sigh, dragging down chimneys and rafters in a thunder of splintered timber.

Every collapse echoed August's unraveling, his grip shattering brick by brick. The house wasn't just falling; it was giving up, devouring itself, leaving no monument behind.

Arthur burst into the courtyard, gulping air like a drowning man just as the floors gave way to a great pit opening below.

The early morning mist clung damply to him, cool against the sweat on his skin. The others huddled in the drive: Alex clutching Theo, Grace and Lance flanking her, Will pacing with his hands in his hair, Julian coughing.

Dust rolled into the sky, thick and choking, turning dawn's pale light the color of smoke. For a moment, the sound was unbearable, like the scream of some dying beast that had haunted the land for generations.

And then—

Silence.

Arthur lowered Colin onto the gravel as if he were made of glass. His own legs threatened to fold, but he forced himself upright again, chest heaving, eyes fixed on the space where his family home had been sitting mere moments ago.

Ashford Manor was gone. Nothing remained but a great hole in the earth and a few crumbling remains of the stone foundation.

Silence fell, heavy and absolute.

Then Theo stirred.

His small body went rigid in Alexandra's arms, and he let free a keening wail that shattered the hush. "I can't—" His voice cracked. "I can't feel him anymore!" He thrashed against his mother's hold, sobbing. "He's gone! Colin's gone!"

Arthur felt hollow at the words, but he forced his voice steady. Dropping to his knees beside Colin, he pressed two fingers to his throat. A faint pulse thrummed back. Relief hit so hard his vision blurred.

"No," Arthur said, shaking him. "No, he's not. Colin?"

For a beat, nothing. Then Colin's lips parted, breath rasping thin and uneven. His eyes fluttered open to reveal solid blackness. Arthur recoiled, but Colin blinked, and Arthur realized that crimson flooded the whites of his eyes, making the normal blue-gray seem darker, like storm clouds choking out the sky.

"Arthur—" His voice was a rasp. He tried to rise, but Arthur caught him. Colin's grip locked onto Arthur's wrist, nails digging in with a strength that didn't belong in so broken a body. For one alarming moment, Arthur thought the bones might snap. Then the grip eased, and Colin sagged back into his arms.

"That sucked," he croaked.

A laugh burst out of Arthur, unsteady and disbelieving. "You absolute moron," he said, far fonder than he meant. "You did it. You pulled Theo free. You broke August's hold."

Colin turned his head toward the ruins, eyes hollow, and winced. "Brought the house down, did I?"

Alexandra gave a short, startled laugh. "You did."

Theo slipped from her arms, creeping forward to press both palms to Colin's chest. His small face pinched in accusation. "I felt you go."

"I know," Colin said, weary. "It's...complicated."

"Complicated how?"

"I'll tell you later." Colin closed his eyes, a long exhale trembling through him. "For now…someone please tell me there's a hospital nearby. Because I feel like hell."

Arthur didn't wait for anyone else to answer. He crouched, slinging Colin's arm across his shoulders. "Up you get."

Colin groaned but didn't resist, sagging against Arthur like a wet sail. Grace darted ahead to throw open the door of their van, her hands shaking as she haphazardly made space for Arthur to climb in, Colin a heap in his lap.

Julian was already in the driver's seat, getting the vehicle started as the rest of the team slowly piled into the vehicle with shell-shocked faces. The engine coughed, then roared to life, and the van lurched forward, leaving the remains of Ashford Manor behind it.

The ride blurred past in a haze of flashing streetlights and muffled directions. Alexandra kept Theo at her side, murmuring promises he was too tired to hear. Grace sat twisted in her seat, eyes flicking constantly to Colin's pallor, her knuckles white around the handle of her door. Every time the van hit a bump, Colin's dead weight jolted against him, a sick reminder of how close he'd come to being truly gone.

Red-and-blue hospital signage cut through the dark like a beacon. They stumbled inside under the wash of antiseptic light, a rush of voices and questions meeting them at the door. Hospital staff swept Colin onto a gurney, and they all trailed after in a stunned, straggling line.

A few hours later, Arthur sat slumped in an unforgiving plastic chair in a waiting room, one knee bouncing as though it could shake loose the tension still coiled inside him. Across the room, Grace and Alexandra murmured. Theo slept fitfully on a nearby bench, his small chest rising and falling under a borrowed blanket. The doctors gave him a clean bill of health, which astonished everyone present. Apparently, Colin had done more than just pull the child free when he'd broken August's connection.

It should have been over. The house was nothing but a pile of rubble and ash. Colin had pulled August's presence free. But he hadn't walked away unscathed.

A door hissed open, and a nurse gave Arthur the look he was learning to hate: wary, apologetic, a little too gentle, as if she'd decided in advance he couldn't handle the truth. "Your friend is stable," she said. "But we're still monitoring the hemorrhages. Several blood vessels burst—in his eyes, his temples, even along his arms. It's... unusual."

Arthur swallowed hard. "Unusual how?"

"We don't see these kinds of ruptures from trauma like you described. A house collapsing would certainly cause damage; broken bones or even impalement are pretty likely. But this looks closer to decompression sickness. Has he recently returned from overseas travel or...I don't know, scuba diving, deep cave exploration?"

Arthur's fingers curled tight against his knees. He remembered Colin standing in the circle, face white with pain, eyes lit from within. He remembered August's shadow passing over him. Pressure. Strain.

"No," he said, at a loss for any way to explain what he knew had caused the damage.

The nurse went on about charts and specialists, but Arthur only half-heard her. He caught Grace's glance, saw her biting her lip, saw Alexandra's worried eyes flick toward Colin's room.

"Can we see him?"

The nurse hesitated, consulting the chart as if the paper might offer an easier answer than her own voice. "One at a time," she said. "He's sedated, but not unconscious. You should know…he might not be quite himself."

Arthur rose before she'd finished, the chair scraping back with a squeal that made Theo stir on the cot. He muttered something reassuring without looking back, his pulse already thundering as he followed her.

The hospital was bright and sterile. Arthur couldn't stop the memory of smoke, of the house crumbling overhead, of Colin limp in his arms. His body still ached from carrying him out.

When the nurse eased open the door, Arthur braced himself.

Colin lay pale against the sheets, the contrast of dark hair and bruised skin making him look otherworldly. Broken blood vessels mapped his arms, with red threads crawling just under the surface.

Arthur stepped closer.

He wanted to call his name, shake him awake, and demand that he not look like this. Instead, he stood staring while the machines hummed, alien in their steadiness compared to the chaos of earlier. For a heartbeat, Arthur thought he saw a flicker pass over Colin's face, not pain, but some kind of awareness.

Colin's fingers twitched against the blanket, as if they were seeking something, and Arthur reached for them without thinking, wrapping his hand around Colin's like an anchor.

"I've got you," he said, though he wasn't sure which of them he was trying to convince.

Behind him, the nurse cleared her throat. "We'll likely have him here for a few more days to reintroduce oxygen levels and hydration. You should know...this could give him lifelong complications."

Arthur didn't answer. He couldn't. He just kept a grip on Colin's hand, as if sheer willpower could keep him safe. "Thank you," he said. He listened as her footsteps retreated, his thumb brushing over the back of Colin's mottled skin. The monitors beeped steadily, a thin reassurance.

For a long time, the machines were the only things that moved. Then Colin called, "Arthur," his voice slurred with pain medication and exhaustion.

Arthur lurched forward, leaning so that he could meet the red-rimmed eyes of the other man. "Yeah, I'm here," he promised, foolhardy and a bit too desperate for his own liking.

Colin nodded and blinked rapidly a few times, like he was trying to get better focus. Arthur watched in icy fear as each blink left his irises black for a few moments before clearing.

CHAPTER 21

THEO

The new house didn't creak the way the manor had. It wasn't full of whispers and sighs. When Theo pressed his ear against the walls, he heard nothing but the faint thrum of pipes and the occasional scuff of branches brushing the siding outside. The air smelled of wet paint and pine-scented floor cleaner. It was bright and alive.

Sunlight spilled through the clear windows and stretched in warm squares across the honey-colored floorboards, softening the corners of the rooms. Dust motes drifted lazily in the beams, glittering like suspended stars. Beyond the glass, the world was loud with normal things like cars groaning down the street, a dog barking, and the tinkling of wind chimes. Theo stopped in the still-bare living room and let the heat soak into his skin like proof he wasn't dreaming.

"Watch out, Kiddo!" Lance's voice rang out, pulling him from his thoughts.

Theo darted out of the way just as Lance turned the corner with a teetering stack of boxes labeled *Kitchen*, his eyes barely visible over the wobbling tower. He staggered into the room and dropped them with a grunt on the island counter.

Theo moved to the front door, where his mom stood like a foreman at a construction site. She had her sleeves rolled up and her hair pulled into a messy knot, clipboard in hand, ticking boxes as Will and Julian shouldered furniture through the threshold. "Come on," she teased as Uncle Arthur grunted, hefting a box marked *Books*. "I thought you were stronger than this."

Uncle Arthur muttered something under his breath as he shuffled past her into the house.

Theo glanced back into the living room, where Colin had claimed a patch of floor, shoulders pressed against the wall and eyes half-lidded. He hadn't lifted a single box yet, and nobody had asked him to. It had been three weeks since the chaos of Ashford Manor—nineteen days, to be exact. Theo had been counting them carefully. He wasn't sure how many it would take for it all to fade from nightmares to bad memories, but keeping track felt important.

The hospital released Colin just a few days ago. He still had deep purple marks under his eyes and a rim of red around his left iris. The worst were the lines running up his arms, like an intricate map of the damage August Ashford had done. He tired easily, and nobody had said anything, but his left arm hung differently at his side, like he couldn't quite feel it right. Theo hated that nobody had told him exactly what was wrong, especially since he could see more than they could now.

Colin tilted his head to watch as Will and Julian wrestled a sofa through the open entry, the legs scraping against the doorframe with a teeth-gritting squeal.

Julian let out a low whistle as they finally muscled the sofa into place and stood back, hands on hips. "Damn, this place is great. I can't believe you were gonna stay on the estate when you could afford this baby."

Theo's mom glanced over from the doorway, a strand of hair slipping loose. "Well, we've got the manor to thank for that." She checked something off her clipboard. "The insurance payout for a completely collapsed building because of structural damage is substantial."

"Structural damage," Will scoffed.

Arthur's voice floated from the kitchen, where he was already rummaging through cabinets. "Well, it's not like we could put 'father's possessed spirit' on the insurance forms."

Julian snorted. "Still, I didn't expect the payout to cover all this. Feels like some kind of good karma, getting something this good out of that disaster."

"It wasn't just the house," Will said, brushing dust from his palms. His eyes flicked to Colin, lingering for a beat. "We all paid for it. Some more than others."

Colin gave a faint shrug, only his right shoulder lifting, and his gaze slid to the window where sunlight streamed in golden and relentless. He didn't answer.

"Anyway," Theo's mom said briskly, shifting the mood, "it was enough to make sure you all got paid and to put a roof over Theo's head. I'll take it."

The screen door croaked open and banged shut again. Grace stepped through in a wash of sunlight, a laundry basket hooked in her arms. It overflowed with tangled cords, routers, and chargers spilling over the rim like wild vines. The bright red scarf holding her curls back gleamed against her brown skin. Without ceremony, she dumped the basket into Julian's arms.

"This is your problem now."

Julian nearly dropped the heap and shot her a flat look. "Aye, aye, cap'n," he deadpanned, giving a crooked salute before disappearing down the hallway with the mess clutched against his chest.

Grace brushed her palms against her jeans and crossed to Colin and crouched so she was on his level, her voice slipping under the surrounding clamor. "You holding up okay?"

Colin blinked, as if he hadn't expected to be noticed. Then he lifted one shoulder in a half-shrug and rasped, "Just holding up this wall for you."

"Good," Grace replied simply, with no pity in her tone. "That's your job today. Supervising. Make sure those two idiots don't put the sofa under the window where the glare'll fry the TV." She jerked her chin toward Will and Arthur, who were arguing as usual.

Colin's lips twitched—the faintest suggestion of a smile, but it was there. Grace stood, clapped her hands briskly, and turned toward Theo's mom. "Alright. Where do you want me next?"

The crew scattered again: Grace, Lance, and Will clattered back down the porch steps to fetch more boxes, Mom trailing behind them with her clipboard.

Theo started toward his new bedroom, only to pause at the sound of Uncle Arthur's heavy footsteps crossing the room. Arthur lowered himself onto the floor beside Colin with a loud, theatrical groan, exaggerating the weight on his joints. He leaned his broad shoulder just enough into Colin's space, not quite a hug, but contact all the same.

From where Theo lingered in the doorway, he couldn't hear the words, but he could see Colin's defensive posture—the way his arms folded tight, his mouth pressed thin.

"I'm fine, Arthur," Colin said eventually, pitched loud enough for him to catch. His tone was sharp but tired, stripped of bite. "I know you feel you have to check in out of guilt, but—"

"It's not guilt, idiot," Arthur cut in, sighing. He said the word the same way Lance called Theo *Kiddo* or Will called him *Champ*, a term worn soft by use.

Colin huffed, eyes closing briefly. "I really am okay. I mean—I'm not. Obviously. But I will be fine."

Arthur studied him for a long moment, the silence filled only by the thud of boxes on the porch and Grace laughing outside. "Can you at least promise to tell me if you start to feel dizzy?"

Colin's mouth quirked, teasing. "I solemnly swear I'll tell you if I need anything or feel the slightest bit off."

"Thank you." Arthur pushed himself up smoothly, ignoring Colin's eye roll at the unnecessary theatrics, and strode back out into the daylight.

The house seemed suddenly hollow without the others' noise. Theo glanced back just in time to watch the light shift as a cloud passed, stretching shadows long across the floor. Only they didn't stretch the way they should. The shapes around Colin warped unnaturally, bending at wrong angles, curling toward him like grasping fingers.

Theo froze. His pulse thundered in his ears.

Colin's shoulders locked tight. His head bowed, and a tremor rippled down his frame. Shadows pooled deeper, swelling like ink in water, curling around him in a suffocating embrace. His fists clenched, jaw rigid, breath dragging rough and uneven. Then he shuddered violently, and the dark tendrils snapped back into place. The room was still again.

Theo's chest ached with the effort of not moving, not speaking. He should have looked away, pretended he hadn't seen. But when Colin finally raised his head, their gazes collided. The silence between them was thick, stitched with everything Theo didn't know how to say.

Colin's mouth twitched—not quite a smile, not quite a frown, something in between. A surrender.

"You okay, Theo?" His voice was thin, almost normal.

Theo's throat tightened. He bit his lip. "Are you?"

The air smelled of paint and dust and pine cleaner: normal things, safe things. But beneath it, Theo swore he could taste the cold, metallic tang of Ashford Manor again. He swallowed hard.

No one would believe him. Maybe no one *could*. But he knew the truth: August Ashford hadn't died in the ruins. He'd found a new home.

Inside Colin.

And Colin was still fighting.

Theo pressed his fists against his ribs, trying to ease the fear lodged there. The question that burned wasn't whether Colin could win—it was how long he could keep winning.

www.ingramcontent.com/pod-product-compliance
Lightning Source LLC
Chambersburg PA
CBHW070337130626
46556CB00007B/2896